PFB/48920/10
GB/G/9
R/EC

Oxford in Asia Modern Authors

Rope of Ash

Rope of Ash
(Rentong)

SHAHNON AHMAD

Translated and introduced by
HARRY AVELING

Kuala Lumpur
OXFORD UNIVERSITY PRESS
Oxford New York Melbourne
1979

Oxford University Press
OXFORD LONDON GLASGOW
NEW YORK TORONTO MELBOURNE WELLINGTON
KUALA LUMPUR SINGAPORE JAKARTA HONG KONG TOKYO
DELHI BOMBAY CALCUTTA MADRAS KARACHI
NAIROBI DAR ES SALAAM CAPE TOWN

© *Oxford University Press 1979*

All rights reserved. No part of this publication may be reproduced, stored in a retrieval system, or transmitted, in any form or by any means, electronic, mechanical, photocopying, recording or otherwise, without the prior permission of Oxford University Press

ISBN 0 19 580441 4

Printed in Singapore by Koon Wah Lithographers
Published by Oxford University Press, 3, Jalan 13/3,
Petaling Jaya, Selangor, Malaysia

Contents

Introduction vii
A Note on the Translation xvii
1. THE TORCH 1
2. THE WOUNDED BULL 20
3. DAY INTO NIGHT 40
4. BURN! BURN! 58
5. THE TIGER 94

Introduction

Rentong is the third of Shahnon Ahmad's novels to appear in English translation. *No Harvest but a Thorn*, a translation by Adibah Amin of *Ranjau Sepanjang Jalan*, was first published in 1972; *Srengenge*, from the novel of the same title, is to be published in 1979. *Rentong* (1965), was, however, Shahnon Ahmad's first full-length work and is essential to an appreciation of the development of this major Malay author.

Shahnon Ahmad was born on 13 January 1933, in the village of Banggul Derdap, Sik district, on the mountainous edge of the Kedah-Perlis rice bowl. After completing his primary education in Sik, he proceeded to Sultan Abdul Hamid College, Alor Star, where he completed the Cambridge School Certificate in 1953. After premature retirement from the Royal Malay Regiment because of an accident, he taught English, and the Malay Language and Literature, in various schools in north Malaya between 1955 and 1967.

Shahnon's first collection of short stories was an anthology of translations, *Setanggi* (Incense); this was followed by two volumes of his own stories, *Anjing-anjing* (Dogs, 1964) and *Debu Merah* (Red Dust, 1965). The novels began to come in quick succession: *Rentong* (1965), *Terdedah* (Exposed, 1965), *Ranjau Sepanjang Jalan* (1966), *Protes* (Protest, 1967), *Menteri* (The Minister, 1967), *Perdana* (The Prime Minister, 1969)

Srengenge (1973), *Sampah* (Rubbish, 1974), *Kemelut* (Crisis, 1977) and *Seluang Menodak Baung* (The Carp Spearfish the Bass, 1978). A further collection of short stories was published in 1978 in Malay, *Selesai Sudah*; and an English translation, *The Third Notch*, is currently in press. His works have been honoured extensively in Malaysia, and their steady translation into English attests to the growing international recognition that is being paid to them.

Although Shahnon could probably live on the basis of his royalties, he has continued to study and teach. In 1971 he was awarded the degree of Bachelor of Arts in Asian Studies from the Australian National University; in 1975, his study of the Obscure Poetry movement in Malay poetry led to the award of the degree of Master of Arts from the Universiti Sains Malaysia, Penang, where he now serves as Dean of the School of Humanities. He completed the pilgrimage to Mecca in 1978 and bears the title *Haji*.

Shahnon's career, if not his spectacular success, is typical of many Malay authors of the post-war period. He began writing as a young man, after an education partly in Malay and partly in English. He was engaged in a middle-class, professional occupation, teaching, which kept him in close contact with Malay society. His position encouraged in him a sense of responsibility for the improvement of the standing of that community. One may contrast this profile of post-war Malay writers with the typical post-war Indonesian author, who was, in many cases, of aristocratic origin, and educated almost exclusively in Dutch. Many post-war Indonesian authors were not only strongly influenced by European literature, they had often had the opportunity to spend a lengthy period of residence abroad. Their occupations tended to be bureaucratic or self-employed, and their residence was almost exclusively in Jakarta. There was, in the 1950s, little sense of responsibility among Indonesian authors for shaping social change in the countryside, nor did writers see themselves as spokesmen for their particular ethnic group. Malay writing was modest, easily understood, widely accepted, and tended to be didactic; Indonesian writing was sophisticated, sometimes difficult to understand (especially for the outsider), read by a small circle, and tended to be private and personal.

During the 1950s, Malay writing was centred in Singapore. The so-called 'Generation of the Fifties' explicitly saw themselves as committed writers. Caught up in the increasing demands for independence from colonial rule, they favoured two areas of subject matter in their prose: the Malays as an oppressed urban community, and Malays as a socially divided rural community, exploited by other races and foreign capital. Although Ishak Haji Muhammad had already observed in his *Anak Mat Lela Gila* (The Son of Mad Mat Lela, 1941; English translation in press) that the Singapore Malay was a different person from his Peninsula counterpart, he left no doubt that this toughness and resilience was due to the more demanding conditions of the fiercely competitive Lion City. These conditions were explored extensively in the short stories of the 1950s, and they form the basis of the Generation's most important novel, *Salina*, by A. Samad Said, a journalist and former hospital orderly.

Siti Salina is a prostitute. She lives in a *kampung*, or residential area, which is nothing more than a converted collection of goat-stalls, facing a Public Works Department barracks across a dirty track. The *kampung* is served by a common ablutions block, which is protected during the day by a Sikh watchman. Salina works to keep a slouch called Abdul Fakar, who spends most of the day sleeping, and most of the night spending Salina's money at any of a number of entertainment parks, dance halls or 'midnights' (film screenings). Despite her unsavoury occupation, and her delusion that Abdul Fakar is her, now dead, childhood sweetheart, Siti Salina is a woman of considerable refinement and sensitivity, who has been forced to suffer because of the effect of the Second World War on her family. She is particularly kind to a newcomer to the *kampung*, Hilmy, who hopes one day to be an architect, and to the young girl, Nahidah. Salina eventually recovers from her delusions and mends her ways, but most of the other characters come to settle for less than satisfactory lives. Hilmy's ambitions are abandoned when his mother, a washerwoman, dies. Nahidah, first employed as a waitress in a coffee shop, then raped by Abdul Fakar, finally drifts into a rather miserable marriage to a waterside worker, at a time of widespread industrial unrest. The *kampung* is burned down and its members dispersed.

In the novel, Samad Said suggests three possible ways of escape from this urban hell. The first is religion: however, the religion of the old man, Haji Karman, is self-righteous, unsuited to helping people in their present difficulties in this world, and more than somewhat self-deluding. (Salina herself makes these comments.) The second escape is to return to the purer world of the countryside, and Salina and another girl do actually spend some time in Kelantan, before Salina is drawn back to the city again. The third way out, the most successful and yet the most difficult to secure, is English education. (In one place in the novel, one of the character dismisses the Malay school certificate as suitable for wrapping fish-paste, but nothing more!)

The full effect of an English education is vividly conveyed in the English short story entitled 'A Common Story', by a Malay graduate of the University of Malaya in Singapore. Yusuf goes to Singapore 'to learn, to be enlightened, as they say'. His Singapore becomes 'Beethoven at one end and Bill Haley at the other. In between, there was Hemingway, the *Week-Ender*, blue films, lovemaking in the parks, prostitution in the back lanes, democracy in Assembly House, the voice of freedom rolling out of River Valley Road', and other, more radical political ideas as well. Although he could have stayed and been 'a journalist of some kind or made a fortune in the Malayan Civil Service', Yusuf shocks and disappoints his parents by turning his back on all that the city can offer an English educated Malay, and wanting to go back to the coarse life of the padi-planters and the rubber-tappers in his village. Trying to justify himself to a friend, Yusuf says, 'I think I know. I've lost my soul. That's it, I've lost my soul. Do you know what I mean? I must go back there. That's where I belong. My life's bound up with the people there. I must go back and learn their language again, learn their ways and live with them. Maybe then I'll get back my soul.'

From Singapore, a place of sin and degradation, where the Malay community had little opportunity for self-advancement from the bottom of the heap, the countryside seemed, to authors, to offer enormous possibilities. The community was largely self-contained. Islam was practised, sometimes superstitiously, but nevertheless, devoutly believed in. The air was fresh, the scenery was green, beautiful, and gentle. Granted the differences between the very rich and the very poor, which might occasionally keep a devoted couple apart (such as Uda and Dara in Usman Awang's famous short story), at least one knew the system and how to adjust to it. The obligation to 'go back' became a constant theme, and has remained so. (Azizi Haji Abdullah's *Senja Belum Berakhir*, Unfinished Twilight, is a fairly recent example.)

In Shahnon Ahmad's case, however, he had never really been away. The son of a headman, he had continued to teach in the rural areas. Further, he began writing at a time when the Malay community was turning away from its sense of economic and political infer iority and starting to demand a larger share in the management of the newly founded Malaysia. The French literary sociologist, Lucien Goldmann, has argued that writers articulate not their own private view of reality, but the 'world view' of the social group to which they choose to align themselves. (A world view is 'a way of seeing and feeling a concrete universe of beings and things', 'a coherent and unitary view of reality'.) The author expresses, through his work, the world view of his group with particular depth and coherence. The Generation of the Fifties presented their perception of the Malay community from their own position of weakness in the city, and found it often necessary to use romantic fantasy and other means of self-comfort. Shahnon, in the predominantly Malay north of the peninsula, at a time of increasing community self-awareness, presents a far more realistic and self-assertive view. In his work, to be Malay is to be rural. The values of the authentic Malay are quiet determination, the ability to solve one's problems without doing violence to tradition, and the careful evolution of a self-contained community. The deviant values are undirected aggression and the desire to destroy the harmony of the society one lives in.

Readers of *No Harvest but a Thorn* will remember the stark presentation of an isolated family in the remote mountain village of Banggul Derdap, resolutely struggling to farm their rice. The power of the novel derives from the archetypal strength of the peasant continuously defending his crop from overwhelming natural odds. There is a strong submission to Islam: 'Life and death', the novel begins, 'dearth and plenty, are in the hands of God. In the hands of *Allah* the Almighty.' Yet there is also a recognition of an alternate system of belief in spirits and taboos. 'Lahuma was shocked at his wife's words', we read on page thirty-six. 'Drought. Flood. Crabs. *Tiaks*. Why was his wife suddenly so bold, mentioning those evils by name? Lahuma would never say those names aloud; it was taboo. Perhaps all those disasters would actually befall them this year.' They do, and worse—Lahuma dies, his wife goes mad. But the community is caught in its own problems and its own search for the solutions to these essentially insoluble problems. In *Srengenge*, the same impression of the village is given, now not as conflict between man and nature, but between man and the supernatural. The split between orthodox Islamic belief and animistic practices is strengthened in this work. If the novel ends with the chanting of the thirty-sixth *surah* of the Quran, 'Yāssin', on death and the day of judgement, there is, nevertheless, the very real sense that the spirit of the mountain has been only temporarily appeased by the sacrifice of ritual objects and the death of the old man.

Rope of Ash is set in the same village as these other two novels: the fictional village of Banggul Derdap, with its fields, houses and mosque. In the background of the novel is the annual rhythm of the planting, replanting, growth and harvest of the rice crop. The village is defined as a community of a few families, both strongly dependent on, yet fiercely independent from, each other. Shahnon does not see the village in any falsely sentimental way; he graphically presents the emotional tensions that can exist and grow unchecked among a small group of people. The characters are clearly delineated: Pak Senik, the village headman, a man of justice and infinite patience, unwilling to solve problems by forcing others to accept the right solution for reasons they do not understand; Dogol, the manipulator, who almost destroys all Pak Senik believes in by his deceit, his selfishness, and his wilful insistence on violent means; and Semaun, the sturdy youth, who is forced to defend his family from the villagers' hatred, and who is accused of repeating a campaign of violence waged by his father many years ago. The theme of social change lies behind the novel: the government is prepared to give Banggul Derdap extensive assistance if the villagers will all agree to plant two crops a year instead of the traditional one. This theme, potentially so propagandistic, is never blatant; it becomes, rather, a simple, everyday consideration to be worked out the best way everyone can. Shahnon is much more concerned with telling an exciting story. The suspense at the end of the story, where it seems possible Semaun may shoot Dogol, Dogol may shoot Pak Senik, or the tiger might kill any one of them, is very competently handled indeed. The final resolution is as much a triumph of grim necessity as it is a victory for the principle of rural cooperation for agricultural development.

Shahnon's later work grapples with the ambiguities of Malay politics (*Menteri* and *Perdana*), and with the emergence of a rich, urban Malay élite, determined to settle permanently in the city (*Selesai Sudah*). The member of parliament (*wakil rakyat*) and the indigenous (*bumiputera*) businessman appear as new and important characters in his writing, in line with further changes in the socio-economic and political structure of Malay society in the late 1960s and the 1970s. This is not the place to discuss these works.

Everything in Shahnon's writing must be set against the imaginary world of Banggul Derdap, and to begin to know Banggul Derdap, one must begin with *Rope of Ash*. The strength, patience, hatred, violence, faith, superstition, desire for social change, and respect for what is valuable in the old, that characterizes Shahnon Ahmad's work as a whole, starts with this first novel.

Perth, Albany
1978

Swami Anand Haridas
(Harry Aveling)

Works Referred to in the Introduction

Malay
(Place of publication Kuala Lumpur, unless otherwise specified.)

Azizi Haji Abdullah, *Senja Belum Berakhir*, Pustaka Nasional, Singapore, 1971.
Ishak Haji Muhammad, *Anak Mat Lela Gila*, Federal Publications, Singapore, fifth printing, 1975.
Shahnon Ahmad, *Anjing-anjing*, Jambatan Mas, 1964.
———, *Debu Merah*, Abbas Bandung, Melaka, 1965.
———, *Rentong*, Abbas Bandung, Melaka, 1965, second printing, 1968.
———, *Terdedah*, Abbas Bandung, Melaka, 1965.
———, *Ranjau Sepanjang Jalan*, Utusan Melayu Bhd., 1966.
———, *Protes*, Abbas Bandung, Melaka, 1967.
———, *Menteri*, Dinas Penerbitan Pustaka Sekolah, Alor Setar, 1967.
———, *Perdana*, Pustaka Nasional, Singapore, 1969.
———, *Srengenge*, Dewan Bahasa dan Pustaka, 1973.
———, *Sampah*, Dewan Bahasa dan Pustaka, 1974.
———, *Kemelut*, Utusan Publications, 1977.
———, *Selesai Sudah*, Heinemann Educational Books, Asia, 1977.
———, *Seluang Menodak Baung*, Heinemann Educational Books, Asia, 1978.
Usman Awang, 'Uda dan Dara', in *Mekar dan Segar*, Asraf (ed.), Oxford University Press, 1959.

Translations of Malay Works into English
(By Harry Aveling, unless otherwise specified.)

A. Samad Said, *Salina*, Dewan Bahasa dan Pustaka, 1975.
Ishak Haji Muhammad, *The Son of Mad Mat Lela*, Federal Publications, Singapore (in press).

Shahnon Ahmad, *The Third Notch*, Heinemann Educational Books, Asia (in press).

Shahnon Ahmad, *No Harvest but a Thorn* (Translated by Adibah Amin), Oxford University Press, 1972.

Shahnon Ahmad, *Srengenge*, Heinemann Educational Books, Asia, 1979.

Usman Awang, 'Uda and Dara', in *ASEAN Short Stories*, R. Yeo (ed.), Heinemann Educational Books, Asia, (in preparation).

Other References in English

George Herbert, 'The Collar', in *The Metaphysical Poets*, H. Gardner (ed.), Penguin Books, Harmondsworth, 1957.

Kassim Ahmad, 'A Common Story', in *Twenty-two Malaysian Stories*, L. Fernando (ed.), Heinemann Educational Books, Asia, 1968.

L. Goldmann, *Towards a Sociology of the Novel* (Translated by A. Sheridan), Tavistock Publications, London, 1975.

A Note on the Translation

I have tried to present a simple, tight translation, that represents the world of Banggul Derdap in as immediately accessible a manner as possible. Three matters require comment.

The original Malay title, *Rentong*, means 'burnt to a cinder', 'charred black'; the word is used a number of times in the fourth chapter, when the villagers decide to burn Semaun's house. The short word carries a good deal of impact in Malay that none of the literal translations seem to hold, so I have sought an alternative title. The phrase 'no harvest but a thorn', used as the title of a previous translation of a novel by Shahnon Ahmad, comes from the English writer George Herbert's poem 'The Collar'. I have taken another phrase from that poem—'Forsake thy cage,/Thy rope of sands,/Which pettie thoughts have made, . . .' and adapted it for the title of this English translation.

The religious titles, Imam and Lebai, have been for the greater part left untranslated. The Imam is the Presiding Elder, or the Prayer Leader of the Muslim congregation during the Friday prayers; he is also responsible for regulating the calendar with regard to times of ritual observance, and for deciding obscure points of doctrine. The Lebai, according to Wilkinson's *Malay-English Dictionary*, are 'a class of persons of Southern Indian descent and connected by family association with tell-

gion. . . . They are expected to be pillars of the mosque and are invited to charitable and religious feasts.'

Contrary to my practice in translating *Srengenge*, I have left unchanged the familiar titles Pak (Father), Mak (Mother) and Tok (honorary form of address for elderly men); the reader may decide which is the more effective.

1
The Torch

Night had scarcely begun. The remote rural district was already wrapped in profound silence; the sort of silence that pierces clear through a man's mind and the deepest recesses of his heart. Sometimes the silence was briefly broken; broken by the water in a rice-field rippling, as a greedy mudfish pursued its offspring. And, at other times, there was the faint call of a pheasant from the middle of the forest which half surrounded the isolated village. But neither the mudfish in the fields nor the pheasants in the forest were ever very persistent. And the isolated rural district was soon wrapped in sharp, inescapable silence once again.

Jusoh was outside. He sat on the platform made of bamboo poles at the front of his house, dangling his feet and letting his rice settle. The leaf cigarette clenched in his mouth glowed like a tiny coal. As his mouth puffed the smoke out, he cast his gaze over the extensive ricefields spread before him. Although the moon had not yet risen, Jusoh could inwardly visualize each square of land that lay in front of him. There was one thing he was very conscious of. The fields were flooded. In a few days, the villagers would take their tools and start weeding. If nothing went wrong, he too would join them. Suddenly, Jusoh's thoughts were interrupted by the sight of a torch of dry fronds in the distance. The torch bounced up and down, as though the man carrying it were walking like a crow. Jusoh threw the grey butt of the cigarette to the ground. He stretched his neck, trying to guess to whom the crow-like gait belonged. But he said nothing. His eyesight was very bad nowadays.

'Siti!'

His wife rushed out.

'Who do you think that is?'

Siti moved to the front of the platform. She peered into the dark.

'Who do you reckon?' Jusoh repeated.

'The Tok Imam walks like that,' Siti replied. 'If it isn't the Imam, it must be Lebai Debasa. The Imam and Lebai Debasa are the only two people in Banggul Derdap who walk like a droop-horned water-buffalo. How many people has the headman invited tonight?'

'Is he jumping up and down?' Jusoh asked, ignoring his wife's question.

'How many people did Pak Senik invite tonight?' Siti insisted.

Jusoh was as silent as a rock, although his wife's comparison of the two men to a droop-horned buffalo amused him greatly. The Imam was a very large man. He had a good deal of flesh on him. It sometimes took him almost four minutes to climb up into the pulpit.

'Why are there always so many meetings?' Siti asked, once she decided that he was not going to answer her previous question.

'Why do you think?' Jusoh replied. 'Someone is always testing his horns. There have been quarrels for as long as anyone can remember, even if the village is no bigger than a monkey's instep. It used to be Pak Kasa. He'd take a swing at anyone. He almost skinned a man alive one time for putting a boundary marker in the wrong place. He used to go stark raving mad if anyone touched his irrigation channels. If he couldn't find the person involved, he'd attack their animals. It looks as though Semaun has inherited his father's evil ways. Last month one of Dogol's cows was hamstrung. That damned Semaun must have done it.'

Siti let the conversation die. The thought of how badly Pak Kasa had behaved many years ago revolted her. Not only could he never get on with any of the villagers, but he actually went about crippling their beasts as well. As though the innocent animal was no more than a weed in a rice-field.

The torch had moved further away. The droop-horned buffalo gait was no longer as obvious. Then, at a corner of the sunset side of the fields, another torch appeared. The flame burnt so strongly that there was no mistaking the bearer.

'Ah! That's Dogol,' Siti confidently announced to her husband.

'Our headman is an angel,' Jusoh said, totally uninterested in the news of Dogol's torch. 'If it had been me, I'd have shoved Semaun in jail long ago. There's no point having a swine like that in the village.'

'Why doesn't Pak Senik report him to the government?'

'I've already told you that,' replied Jusoh. 'Our headman's an angel. He doesn't want to get anyone into trouble. And he doesn't want the other villages to talk about us either. He'd rather solve things himself. But Semaun isn't one of us anymore. He belongs in jail. Not here in the village. . . . Get my torch from the kitchen. Pak Senik will be waiting for me.'

Siti obediently went back inside the house. While waiting for the torch of dry fronds, Jusoh left the bamboo platform and made for the sleeping quarters. Stepping over the threshold, he kicked a number of sweaty pillows out of his way, against the wall. He snatched his fez and jacket from the hook. Then he returned outside again. Siti stood on the platform with a three-foot length of torch in her hand. An oil lamp was burning at the top of the stairs. She lit the fronds. The flame leapt up, as though she had poured petrol on it. After rolling his sarong tightly around his waist, Jusoh started to leave the house. He paused briefly on the first step. His mouth moved as though he was reciting the prayer for protection against poisonous snakes. And once the prayer was finished, he continued walking. Siti followed him with her eyes, until he passed through the bamboo fence dividing his houseland from the expanse of rice-fields.

Jusoh strode along the muddy rice-field walls. Small frogs, half covered with dew, leapt off the soft walls and into the water, as though frightened that Jusoh's hard, calloused feet might kick them. There was an occasional stirring of the water as a mudfish swam after its offspring. But Jusoh ignored the tiny creatures of God. There was no time to waste. Pak Senik and the senior men of the village would be waiting for him.

'I wonder if he wants to talk about Semaun?' Jusoh thought, as his gaze darted rapidly up and down the retaining wall.

He wasn't sure why the village headman had called a meeting that night. It was true the headman never liked to draw too much attention to controversial issues, especially when the matter concerned his own small village. But Jusoh was sure of one thing: whatever it was, it had something to do with Banggul Derdap. And if it was connected in any way with the village, then he was involved. He quickened his pace again.

Perhaps it was about Semaun hamstringing Dogol's cow, thought Jusoh. But that was an old affair, it had happened over a month ago. Why should he suddenly decide to do something about that now? And if that was the matter in hand, Pak Kasa should have been invited too. He was responsible for all the vicious things that had happened. If Pak Kasa was unable to come out at night, they should have insisted Semaun come instead. Jusoh's blood ran cold at the thought of Semaun. Fear gripped him. Jusoh compared Semaun's large, solid body with his own. His left hand moved to his waist. When he touched the handle of the knife he carried behind him, Jusoh breathed more easily. The knife gave him a measure of courage.

A pheasant screeched in the forest, interrupting his thoughts. Another ten fields to the headman's house. Jusoh felt secure on the long retaining wall. Banggul Derdap had been his home for forty years. He knew every nook and cranny as well as he knew 'Al-Fatihah', the opening words of the Quran. Even without a torch, he would have had no trouble finding his way to the headman's house.

Light spread around him, gradually fading into the darkness. When the night wind whispered in his ears, the flame at the end of the torch twitched like an excited rabbit's ears. The water resting stagnant in the fields to the right and left of him broke into shallow waves. The barely visible tips of the weeds shook back and forth. Jusoh thought of how the villagers would start cutting the weeds in a few days. Then they would drain the water off and harrow the slushy fields. He thought of the bodies of the young men of Banggul Derdap village struggling with the mountain mud. Jusoh was suddenly startled. His heart beat quickly. Something was moving on the retaining wall on the other side of the rice-field. The limited torch light made it impossible to tell what the object was, and whether, in fact, it had shifted at all. The first thing Jusof thought of was Semaun, and his small metal dagger. But why would Semaun want to attack him? He had never done anything to Semaun. Jusoh preferred to live in peace with everybody. But Semaun was not to be trusted. He did exactly as he wanted. When Jusoh remembered how Pak Kasa had run wild ten years ago, he felt even more resentful. Kasa would use his knife on any man's head he thought deserved it, or hamstring a water-buffalo with the same ease another man cut a banana-tree trunk in the swamp for salad filling. Semaun was just as bad.

There were four more fields to the village headman's house. What should he do if he felt the touch of Semaun's knife against his shoulder? Drop, right shoulder first, into the water. His left hand returned to his waist. The old knife was still firmly in place. Jusoh whirled around. He wanted to know who had been following him. If it was Semaun, he would fight him to the bitter end, even though he was sure his short weapon would be no match for the village bully's knife.

He lifted the torch so that its light spread further out. He blinked. The object which had upset him was no longer on the dividing wall. It had vanished. Immediately, he plunged the burning torch into the water. The sound of the fire entering the water made his heart jump.

Jusoh was surrounded by pitch black night. It was so dark he might well have been blind. An oil lamp burnt in the front portion of the headman's house. Jusoh crouched on the embankment, with the short knife held tightly in his right hand. He waited for Semaun to attack.

But there was no attack. Silence fell again. The pheasants were quieter than before. Jusoh sprang up quickly, reassuring himself as he did so. Why was he so obsessed by Semaun's violent character? The stories of Semaun's viciousness had all come from Dogol, but Jusoh believed them implicitly. For some reason he could not explain, the thought of Pak Kasa's cruel nature seemed to take an unnatural delight in disturbing his peace of mind. Jusoh felt cheated; cheated by his own emotions.

'Jusoh!' someone screamed from the direction of the headman's house.

Jusoh bellowed in acknowledgement. The village headman's house was only four small rice-fields' distance away. Jusoh walked towards it in the dark.

On reaching the underneath of the house, Jusoh

straight away washed his legs, rubbing vigorously at the splashes of mud on his calves and ankles.

'Jusoh!' someone called again. It was the village headman's voice. Jusoh recognized its harsh quality at once. Pak Senik had been village headman for ten years.

'Yes,' he replied, walking to the front of the house.

On reaching the stairs, Jusoh groped in the bottom of the round earthenware pot for the long-handled coconut dipper, as though fumbling for a catfish in a puddle in a rice-field. When he found the dipper, he took it out, and poured the water over his feet. He rubbed the sides of his feet along the ground in the same motion one uses to sharpen a razor.

'What happened?' someone else inside the house asked. Jusoh looked up. Dogol, who was sitting well back in a corner of the front part of the house, sniggered.

'I dropped it,' Jusoh said.

'Dropped your torch in the water?' Dogol added.

Jusoh nodded, although nobody would be able to see. The pale light of the oil lamp scarcely reached the stairs.

'We thought you'd been caught by a banshee,' Lebai Debasa butted in, as he leant comfortably against a post in the middle of the room. Jusoh smiled at the remark. He entered the room. Lebai Debasa was a funny man.

'If a banshee had caught me, I'd have brought her along,' Jusoh replied, carrying on the joke. 'Banshees are supposed to be beautiful, aren't they? Fragrant, too. I bet they love pious men.'

His remarks were enthusiastically received. The small room rocked with their laughter. Lebai Debasa shook so hard he had to straighten his white skullcap again. Dogol quivered in his corner like a young bride possessed by a nature spirit. And the fat Tok Imam, who had been lost in a state of contemplation, smiled slightly, revealing his dirty, yellow teeth. Pak Senik, who had been out in the kitchen, suddenly appeared at the door. He looked shocked. His face was covered with amazement.

'A banshee?' he asked.

The question, so clearly indicative of his surprise, was greeted with a howl of laughter. The Imam's smile broadened slightly. Pak Senik came out and sat down.

'I thought Semaun had got you,' he added, wriggling around on the torn, woven mat as he tried to get comfortable.

Their laughter disappeared. The whole atmosphere in the room changed. The flickering light of the oil lamp gave added emphasis to the silence. The Imam wiped the smile from his lips. Jusoh shifted into the middle of the room, almost hitting Lebai Debasa on the back. The mosque official gaped anxiously. Dogol stared fixedly at Pak Senik's nose.

'Has he been making a nuisance of himself again?' Jusoh asked. The thought of the black object he had imagined to be Semaun following him through the fields overwhelmed him with terror. It was the same image that had made him drop his torch. Jusoh's chest tightened.

'I'm sure he knows we're meeting here tonight,' Dogol said. 'He's wicked. And when one of God's creatures turns evil, he can be capable of anything.'

Pak Senik listened quietly.

'How would he know?' Jusoh asked again. Lebai Debasa closed his eyes and swallowed his spittle.

'Someone must have told him,' Dogol replied.

'Of course,' Jusoh said, adjusting his position. He sat bolt upright, with his legs crossed, like a Buddhist monk in front of a corpse. 'The village isn't very big, but you can't trust everybody. Some people will tell you one thing to your face and then say something quite different somewhere else. It isn't easy to find an honest man.'

Tok Imam nodded his head.

'Well?' snapped Debasa. He was completely serious now. 'Someone is trying to divide the village. Who is it? Who? You know who, Pak Senik.'

'Yes, I know,' the headman replied, looking at Dogol. 'So does Tok Imam. But it wouldn't do any good to make a fuss about it. I know everything that happens in Banggul Derdap. I know who's decent and who isn't. I could have the mischief-maker thrown in jail if I wanted to, but I don't. I don't want to use force. I don't want to hurt anyone. I'd rather live in peace. I'm responsible for every single person in the village, including Pak Kasa and his son Semaun.'

Lebai Debasa turned his face away, as though sickened by Pak Senik's continual weakness. Dogol looked at Jusoh. Jusoh sat stunned, like a hen with the plague.

'God doesn't want us to hurt anybody,' the Imam said, breaking his long silence, 'neither our friends nor our enemies.'

Debasa corrected his expression. He looked deep into Tok Imam's face. Pak Senik nodded three times. Dogol groped in the pocket of his long Malay jacket for some cigarette leaves. He sorted through the bundle, straightened the leaves, then pulled one out and flattened it. Squeezing the end, he teased the leaf out, before inserting it in his ear and twisting. Jusoh blinked rapidly. He doubted there could be any finer pleasure in the whole world.

'What if our enemy has hamstrung our cows on two separate occasions?' he asked. The cigarette leaf stopped dancing in his right ear. Dogol took it out and stared at the ragged end for a moment, before throwing it on the ground. Jusoh swallowed hard.

'Lodge a complaint at the Police Station,' Jusoh suggested, once his spittle had come to rest in his belly.

'That would destroy the whole purpose of our meeting here tonight,' Pak Senik said, shaking his head. 'Let's try to avoid a quarrel if we can. Pak Kasa couldn't have cut the cows' hamstrings. And we're not really sure it was Semaun. We don't have any evidence. But even if he did do it, he isn't responsible for all that's happened

Their whole situation is wrong. They never mix with anyone else. They never discuss anything with anyone else. They don't know what's going on. All they know is what happens in their own home. We have to do our best to help them understand.'

'You can teach a fool,' Lebai Debasa cut in, 'but you'll never teach a man who doesn't want to learn, not until the Day of Judgement itself.'

'Coffee, daddy,' a childish voice suddenly said. One of Pak Senik's sons stood gingerly at the door, carrying a tray with five cups of thick black coffee.

The arrival of the coffee killed their discussion. Pak Senik stood up and took the very basic refreshments. He gave each man a cup. Jusoh was first and took the thick black coffee with delight. The cup had no saucer; he placed it carefully on the mat, anxious that his share of what God had seen fit to bestow on them that night should not be spilt and lost.

The night crawled slowly on. The lights which had earlier shone in each of the houses around the rice-fields began to be extinguished one after the other. The villagers were starting to fluff their pillows up, so they could rest their heads after a hard day's work. At dawn, they would return to the fields again. Every last weed had to be dug out. Pak Senik's family, too, had started to make their way to their sleeping quarters. That left only Pak Senik, headman of Banggul Derdap village, Tok Imam, Dogol, Lebai Debasa and Jusoh. They sat facing their cups of hot coffee, waiting for Pak Senik's voice to start the evening's proceedings. Pak Senik still had not officially told them why he had asked them to come. He was an experienced leader. It was better to deal with things one at a time, in an orderly manner. There was nothing to be gained by rushing. Let the rest of the village sleep. Let Banggul Derdap be absolutely still. Let the men finish their coffee first.

'I haven't called you here to talk about Pak Kasa,'

Pak Senik said, shattering the silence. He spoke as though it was the first time he had talked to his guests that evening. Using his right hand, he wiped away the black coffee-grounds from his lips which were cracked in a thousand places. 'Nor did I want to talk about Semaun. Although what I do have to say certainly has some connexion with them.'

His listeners, the four leading men of Banggul Derdap village, were nonplussed. Each man waited for him to continue, especially as Pak Kasa's name had been mentioned. Pak Kasa's name carried the same significance as Semaun's. Semaun represented violence, cruelty and inhumanity. They all hated these traits, except Pak Senik. And only he, of all the people gathered in the front of his house, knew that.

'I want to talk about planting two crops a year,' the headman continued. 'The government will give us seed and fertilizer. They'll supply a tractor, and help pump water out from the river. We have to raise the seedlings and transplant them. We keep the rice. The profits will be four times what we're used to.'

The men were stunned. They had never heard of such a thing.

'Just like that?' Jusoh suddenly asked, as though not believing the village headman.

Pak Senik did not reply. He simply nodded and smiled.

'It sounds too easy,' Dogol whispered to himself, apparently ignoring Pak Senik's nod and his smile. The Imam nodded. He said nothing. His expression showed how pleased he was. He seemed greatly relieved. The effect of Pak Senik nodding his head and Dogol whispering to himself amused Lebai Debasa very much. He burst out laughing, like a madman. Jusoh started to snigger, but when he realized Debasa's laugh was not intended to be humorous, he quickly checked himself. Then he looked at Pak Senik. Pak Senik sat quietly, as though unaware of the mocking thrust of Debasa's laughter.

'Plant twice a year? Free fertilizer? Free seed? Water supplied? Just like that? Just like that?' The questions came pouring out of Lebai Debasa. His eyes moved wildly from Pak Senik's face to that of Tok Imam, and then from him to Dogol, before finally coming to rest on Jusoh. Debasa seemed to be trying to influence them. None of the men made any response.

'We've planted one crop a year for hundreds of years,' Debasa continued, 'and no one ever helped us. Why are they giving us this assistance now?'

'Times have changed,' the Imam interjected quickly.

'Things are different now,' Dogol agreed. 'We have to change too.'

Lebai Debasa turned towards Jusoh. It was clear that he hoped Jusoh would support him. Jusoh immediately destroyed that hope.

'We used to be a colony. Now we're an independent nation.'

Lebai Debasa crumpled on hearing Jusoh's reply. He bowed his head. Quickly taking advantage of the situation, Pak Senik picked up from where he had left off.

'I didn't believe it at first either. No one ever wanted to help us before. But I've gradually come to accept it. There is plenty of proof. A lot of other villages have already received assistance. If we're not careful, we'll miss out altogether.'

Debasa's head remained bowed. His gaze bored its way into the woven screw-pine mat beneath him. He tugged momentarily at the weave with his finger, as though strongly critical of the way Pak Senik's wife had tried to plait the mat. Debasa was well-known for his ready inclination to strongly disagree with other people. Pak Senik had expected him to react in exactly this way. But he was also aware of something else. Lebai Debasa's hostility was never absolute. He would listen to a discussion. He would consider any proof offered. And if he could understand the arguments for a thing, and see the proof for himself, his opposition always rapidly melted. He wasn't like Pak Kasa and Semaun. They would disagree for the sake of it, no matter how untenable they knew their position to be. The thought of Pak Kasa and Semaun led Pak Senik to resume his explanation.

'But there is one condition.'

The short statement was very effective. The Imam blinked. The white cataracts of his eyes stood out clearly, despite the pale light of the lamp. He knew what the condition was. And he knew why they would not be able to meet it.

'We must insist that they drop the condition!' the Imam unexpectedly proposed.

The others were startled. Pak Senik had not even told them what the prerequisite for their receiving the aid was, and yet the Imam was already making his own demands. The four men stared from their different directions. The Imam was surprised.

'What condition?' Lebai Debasa barked angrily.

Before the Imam could reply, Lebai Debasa continued, 'No one has said what the condition is yet. I want to know what is at stake.'

Tok Iman was thrown into confusion. Jusoh coughed, deliberately, as though subtly rebuking the Imam. Dogol sniggered and nodded his head, apparently agreeing with Jusoh's forced cough. The mood on the front verandah of the headman's house eased slightly. The men waited for Pak Senik to speak again.

'Everyone in the village must agree to planting twice a year. If they don't, we won't get a single thing.' The mood changed again. But before his guests could ask him anything, Pak Senik continued, 'The government wants us to work together. They want us to cooperate. To help each other. Neighbours mustn't fight with neighbours. In short, we have to show that we're united before they'll give us any assistance.'

'United in what way?' Lebai Debasa suddenly wanted to know. Pak Senik smiled, as though he had been carefully storing the answer in his head for some time. Perhaps he was pleased that the Lebai had asked something. He was sure that, despite his initial extreme antagonism, Lebai Debasa was slowly beginning to change his attitude.

'Everybody must plant twice a year. Without exception. Everyone. Jusoh, Dogol, you, me . . . all of us.'

'Including Semaun and his family?' Lebai Debasa continued.

They were shocked by the question. Dogol frowned, forming five ridges across his forehead. Jusoh looked hard at the Imam who was still examining the weave of the mat. He understood why the Imam wanted the single condition dropped. Pak Senik nodded in reply.

'It's out of the question!' Jusoh said, shaking his head. 'Out of the question that they'd ever want to cooperate with us.'

'Impossible,' Dogol repeated. 'They can't agree on small things, let alone something as important as this.'

'Semaun's too stuck up,' Jusoh joked. 'He's even more stuck up than Pak Kasa is. He never mixes with the villagers. He never comes to any feasts. He never says hello to anyone. He reaches for his knife at the slightest offence. If anyone says anything wrong to him, he goes stark raving mad. Are we supposed to cooperate with those jinns?'

Pak Senik listened patiently. He was determined to find a peaceful solution, despite his knowledge of Pak Kasa's antics and Semaun's stubbornness. He wouldn't give in. Somehow the two most obstinate men in Banggul Derdap had to learn to live in harmony with everyone else. There were many ways of overcoming their hard-heartedness.

'We mustn't weaken,' Pak Senik said emphatically.

'I'm determined we'll succeed. And that we'll succeed by peaceful means. We mustn't use force; absolutely not.'

Pak Senik's persistent, unmanly chatter made Lebai Debasa feel distinctly uneasy. He had heard it so many times before. Pak Kasa and Semaun weren't like other people; you couldn't expect to sit down and discuss anything in a reasonable manner with them. There wasn't so much as a rice grain of sense in seeking their agreement; they were like wild bulls, always testing their horns.

'There's no way we'll get their consent peacefully,' Lebai Debasa said fiercely. Tok Imam, who had been listening most intently, pouted distastefully.

'We can try,' Pak Senik said.

'Try what?'

'Try and win Pak Kasa over?'

'To planting twice each year?'

Pak Senik nodded.

'Who'll try?' Lebai Debasa continued. His eyes rested briefly on Dogol, then on Jusoh and the Imam.

'All of us,' Pak Senik said softly, not expecting them to agree.

'Me?' Dogol asked, startled. 'They crippled my cow. I don't want to set eyes on them.'

Dogol's aggressive statement made no difference to the calm expression on Pak Senik's face. He pretended not to have heard.

'We have to get the whole village to agree,' Pak Senik said. 'The government wants us to be united.'

Although he realized Pak Senik was deliberately ignoring his previous remark, not a word escaped Dogol's lips. He was silent. His mouth moved slightly, as he struggled to hold back his anger.

'Will you, Jusoh?' the headman asked.

Jusoh jerked, as though someone had stuck a *nibong*[1]

---

[1] A tall tufted palm used for flooring.

thorn in his backside. His swift reaction startled the others.

'Will I what?' Jusoh replied, returning the question.
'Ask Semaun for his agreement?'
'Coax that monster?'
Pak Senik nodded.
'And Pak Kasa as well?'
Again Pak Senik nodded.
'Never!' Jusoh insisted. 'I refuse to crawl to those two monsters. Get someone else.'

Pak Senik did not insist. He would never force anyone to do anything; especially if it was someone whose assistance in administering Banggul Derdap he greatly valued.

'Lebai Debasa?' Pak Senik glanced at the startled mosque official.

'I'll plant twice a year if the government gives us assistance,' Lebai Debasa stated. 'I didn't understand what it was all about before. But I'm sorry, I don't want to go to Pak Kasa's. His family is more dangerous than a giant stinging-nettle. Perhaps the Imam will go.'

'No, I won't!' the Imam immediately exclaimed.

Pak Senik retained his composure. The four rejections had not changed the expression on his face in the slightest. He could tell what lay behind their various answers. None of the villagers liked Pak Kasa. Pak Senik knew that the family had a wild streak, but he didn't like opposing them. He would rather try to find some peaceful solution to all their differences. He didn't want his village looked on with contempt by other villages. Nor did he want himself considered inefficient and unjust.

'I'll do it myself,' he said.

The statement resolved the conflict between the five men. The stolid Imam gulped. He didn't believe the headman would do such a thing. Dogol looked at Lebai Debasa. Lebai Debasa sat rigid. Jusoh had half-rolled a cigarette and stopped what he was doing.

With Pak Senik's statement that he was willing to undertake the task, the meeting was at an end. The men pushed their empty cups into the centre of the verandah.

'If I'm not successful, we'll ask the authorities to consider waiving the rule,' Pak Senik added.

The men nodded. There was nothing more to be said. They were amazed that Pak Senik had offered to try to win over Pak Kasa and his family. Pak Kasa was as dangerous as a jungle trail booby-trapped with pointed bamboo spears. Lebai Debasa couldn't understand it at all. Neither could Jusoh or Dogol; in fact, Dogol blinked several times. He hated the jinns who had hamstrung his cows. None of them said a thing. The Imam was a coward; he was terrified of Semaun's knife hacking its way through his white skullcap. His hasty rejection of the scheme showed how easily he panicked. To be honest, Pak Senik himself wasn't sure he could succeed, although he didn't want the others to know that. He doubted Pak Kasa and Semaun could be convinced of anything. He very much doubted that Pak Kasa would agree to plant twice each year. Pak Kasa never agreed with anyone, it was not in his nature. He was a fighter, and he would fight to the end, even if he destroyed himself in the process. He was willing to accept the consequences. And Semaun had the same blood as Pak Kasa, with, no doubt, the same temperament. Pak Senik knew all that, but he wasn't going to give in so easily. He had to try. He was the headman. He had to think of various strategies he could use to win over Pak Kasa and Semaun. He must go to their house. No matter how violent they were, they wouldn't attack a man without reason. Pak Kasa wasn't an animal. He had a mind. He had a heart. And a man, with a mind and a heart, could never act completely recklessly. He was not like a wounded bull. Pak Senik believed that. And because he did, he was willing to be the one to try to convince Pak

Kasa of the importance of the project.

The Imam leapt to his feet, and snapped his arms out to the side to get his blood moving again. Dogol and Lebai Debasa did exactly the same. They then climbed down the stairs and began lighting their torches. The three torch flames lit up Pak Senik's overgrown front yard. Without saying 'good night', the three men went their separate ways. Pak Senik watched them go. Jusoh had not moved from where he was still sitting cross-legged. When he realized his friends' three torches had long gone, he slowly shook himself.

'Would you mind if I borrowed a flashlight?' he called out to Pak Senik.

Pak Senik turned his eyes away from the burning torches.

'What happened to your torch?'

'I dropped it.'

'Oh! I forgot. The banshee made you drop it.'

Jusoh laughed at Pak Senik's joke. Pak Senik went into the house and returned a few moments later with a large flashlight in his hand. He switched it on and off a few times. The beam shone high into the sky. He held it out for Jusoh to take. Jusoh stood up and took the torch at the same time. After tightening the roll of his sarong around his waist, Jusoh felt ready to go and started down the stairs. Without saying 'good night', he walked across the rice-fields following the same dividing wall he had used before. Pak Senik entered the sleeping quarters but did not close the door. He reappeared with a pillow under his arm. Throwing the pillow on the mat on the front verandah where they had held their meeting, he lay down. For a few moments he rested on his side, staring at the oil lamp which was still alight.

'I must convince Pak Kasa and Semaun of the worth of double planting,' he whispered to himself.

Then he immediately blew the lamp out. Darkness ruled the verandah. Pak Senik adjusted the pillow beneath his head. The night crawled slowly on. It had almost reached its destination. And when it did, another day would begin.

2
The Wounded Bull

Semek usually strolled down to the rice-fields after the dew had dried from the tips of the grass; or even later, if there were a lot of dirty dishes in the kitchen. But that morning she was much earlier. In her left hand was a black kettle, filled with steaming coffee. A broken-handled cup was propped upside down on the spout of the kettle. In her right hand was a small black and white basket. The basket contained a coconut shell's measure of sticky, steamed white rice. Salted, grated coconut had been spread on top of the rice. Three grilled pilchards lay in the middle of the grated coconut.

Semek walked slowly down to the fields, then cautiously stepped onto the still wet dividing walls, aware that if she missed her footing, she would fall into the muddy water and spill the hot coffee and steamed rice which she had prepared for her elder brother. Semek was very fond of her brother. And to prove her love, she had to walk very carefully.

The sky was clear, unlike the last few mornings. The sun's rays shone white on the water in the different fields. Without the bunds, separating one plot from another, the village rice lands would have looked like a single large lake. Many of the villagers were hard at work in their fields as Semek passed with her brother's morning meal. They hacked at the rushes and weeds. But Semek was not interested in the farmers scattered across the various fields. She had eyes only for her brother. He was three acres away, but she could see him clearly. From time to time the water splashed up as his weed-cutter struck home. Small waves rippled across the rice-field. When she reached the field, Semek squatted and put the food on the now somewhat dry retaining wall. She flicked the surface of the water, as though imitating a mudfish chasing its young.

'Brother!' Semek called.

Semaun paused as he swung his weed-cutter. He turned towards the young girl as she splashed the water at the edge of the field. When he realized the girl was his sister, he returned to his task. The food which had been specially prepared for him apparently meant nothing to him. Semek smiled at her brother's stubbornness. She stopped flicking the water and stared at her brother in the middle of the field. She admired the bulging muscles in his broad shoulders and arms. She was lucky to have such a handsome brother. He was the mainstay of the family. Who would look after their fields if Semaun fell sick? Her father was old and often had fits of coughing. Often he could scarcely breathe at all. Her mother only knew how to cook. There was no one else in the world who could help them if they got into difficulty. Pak Senik and his followers had abandoned them a long time ago. Semek wasn't sure what the source of the disagreement was, but she was deeply conscious that none of the other villagers wanted anything to do with her. It had been several years since she was last friendly with any other girls. She was lonely. Her brother, Semaun, was all she had. She could joke with him. She enjoyed his company. What if he fell sick? She didn't want to think of that. Such thoughts would only upset her. Her brother was strong and healthy; he wouldn't get sick easily. She was absolutely sure of that.

'Brother!' Semek called again.

Semaun stopped weeding.

'What?' he shouted back, pretending to be angry.

On hearing his harsh response, Semek pouted. She stuck her tongue out through her pursed lips. Semaun wiped the sweat from his forehead. He was secretly delighted by his adolescent sister's playful cheekiness. She was cute.

'What did you bring me?' Semaun asked, fixing the weed-cutter upright in the mud. The water was shin deep; he waded through it towards where his sister was still squatting. When he was a few feet away from the edge of the field, he scooped some water into his hand and threw it at her. She leapt quickly aside. A couple of drops caught her on the face. She stuck her tongue out further. Semaun laughed.

'Is the sticky rice boiled or steamed?' Semaun asked, as though the small basket might contain other than his favourite food.

Semek went over to her brother and slapped him on his well-rounded shoulder. Semaun's shoulder shook as he laughed. As he waited for his sister to serve the sticky steamed rice and grated coconut onto a spathe of areca-nut palm, Semaun wriggled around, trying to get comfortable. When he at last found a suitable hollow, he sighed with relief. He left his dirty feet hanging in the water. A few large water-buffalo leeches swam about looking for some open wounds in his knotty thighs, but he was not troubled by their presence. Seizing the leeches, he threw them into the middle of the field. Small ripples formed where they landed.

'Has father risen?' Semaun asked his sister.

'Yes,' she replied, putting the dry leaf full of food into his hand.

'Has he had a wash?'

'Not yet.'

'Is he still coughing?'

'He never stops.'

'Did you give him any medicinal lemongrass root?'

'No.'

'Why not?' Semaun asked as he put a handful of rice into his mouth.

'He'd already had some tamarind juice.'

Semaun left off asking questions so he could concentrate on the rice he was chewing. His father had been coughing heavily for the last few months. When the coughing was very bad, the old man's chest became very tight and he could scarcely breathe. A number of *bomohs*[1] had been asked to attend him, but none had ever come. Semaun knew why they hadn't, but had said nothing.

'What about mother?' he asked, once he had swallowed the first handful of rice and grated coconut.

'She's up,' Semek replied. She watched him take the rice in his hand. His muscles rippled each time he rolled the food into a ball to put into his mouth, and the veins stood out on his arms. He had carried her in his strong hands when she was a child. She used to ride on his well-built shoulders. There was a time when he used to carry her on his hip down to the bathing platform. He couldn't do it now. Semek was a young woman. People would have disapproved had they seen her behaving so familiarly with Semaun, even though they were brother and sister.

'When do you want the young shoots ready for transplanting?' she asked, once he had finished his second mouthful.

'When I finish weeding.'

'I thought you were going to turn the ground when you finished weeding.'

'That will only take two days,' Semaun said. 'You can get the shoots ready while I'm doing it.'

'How many bundles do you want?'

'How would I know?' He pretended to be angry.

---

[1] Ritual healers

'You're a woman; you should know. How do you expect to get married if you don't know a thing like that?'

Semek jumped up and down on the retaining wall, then pounded him on the back in revenge. Semaun laughed heartily. When Semek realized she was making no impression, she stopped punching him.

'What about you, anyway?' she snapped.

'What about me?'

'You're old enough to be married. Why aren't you?'

'I am not old. Who said I was? You?'

Snatching up the basket, Semek started walking home, leaving the kettle of hot coffee behind. Semaun laughed as he watched her walk away. She was growing up. In a few years she would be even more grown up. When she was old enough, the young men would come asking for her hand. Semaun didn't know exactly who would ask for her. But there was one thing he was sure of: none of the young men in Banggul Derdap would dare ask for her hand. He was certain of that. But he wasn't worried by so much as a grain of rice. There were a lot of young men in the world. He wanted his sister to live in peace when she married. They would divide the five fields between them. Half for Semek and half for himself.

Semaun jumped up after finishing his cup of coffee and waded back to the middle of the field. Pulling the weed-cutter out of the water, he started swinging it energetically again. He wanted to finish the field that morning, so he could let the water stand for at least a day. After the roots rotted, he would knock a hole in the embankment. He wanted to let the field drain before he started turning the ground. And once he started harrowing, he would get Semek to pick the young rice plants. He wanted to plant the field with *serindit* rice. It was a hardy variety.

His fantasies were suddenly interrupted by a faint

voice in the distance. Semaun stopped swinging his weed-cutter. For several moments he stood like a rock in the middle of the muddy water.

'Brother!' The gentle voice came from the direction of his house. The term was a common one in the village, but no one, except Semek, ever addressed Semaun that way. She took a delight in teasing her strong, handsome brother. Semaun ignored her and started cutting the weeds again.

'Brother! Brother! Come home! Come home!' The soft, firm voice repeated itself over and over. Semaun turned around again.

He immediately caught sight of someone rushing along the dividing walls towards him. By the red scarf streaming behind her, he could tell it was Semek. She was running very quickly, as though a mad dog was after her. Semaun was amazed. He waited anxiously to hear what she had to say.

His father was probably having trouble breathing, Semaun thought to himself. Why hadn't they massaged him with oil? Where was his mother? He waded to the edge of the field, leaving his weed-cutter upright in the middle of the water.

'What's wrong?' he asked her anxiously.

Semek was exhausted. She was breathing too heavily to be able to answer his question at once. He grabbed her by the hand.

'What's wrong?' he demanded. He was impatient for the news locked up inside her. Something bad must have happened. Her face showed how worried she was.

'What's wrong?' he screamed, unable to restrain himself any longer. He squeezed her hand tightly. She put her mouth to his ear and whispered something.

'Pak Senik came.'

'When?' Semaun asked, once Semek had finished.

'He just arrived.' She was still panting.

'Who's with him?'

'He's on his own.'
'What does he want?'
'I don't know.'
'Who sent you to get me?'
'Father.'

Semaun jumped into the water and waded out to his weed-cutter. Snatching the implement up, he placed it across his broad shoulder, before wading back again to the edge of the rice-field. Semek waited for him on the narrow embankment, shaking like a sick hen. Then he strode off, with his sister following behind him. His wet sarong was full of mud. The mud trickled down his thighs and onto the ground, leaving splashes of dirty water in the hairs of his legs. He muttered as he walked. Something was wrong. What did Pak Senik want? No one had crossed their threshold for years.

Perhaps he has come to arrest me, Semaun thought to himself. He quickened his pace. If so, Pak Senik would find it harder than taking rice off a plate. Semaun tightened his grip on the handle of the weed-cutter. Perhaps he had come because of Dogol's cow. But that was an old thing. It happened more than a month ago. And, anyway, Semaun felt he was in the right. Dogol was the guilty one. The government had given every person in Banggul Derdap village one cow each. His family had got nothing at all. Why not? Dogol only worried about himself. Semaun lived in Banggul Derdap, didn't he? He had done nothing wrong. Laying a charge against an innocent man could have very serious consequences. Semaun would go to the Police Station, but not before he'd sunk his weed-cutter into Dogol's shoulder, or anyone else who tried to interfere with him.

'Don't frown like that,' Semek said from by his side. 'Perhaps he wants to help us.'

Semuan did not reply, although he had heard what she said. He continued walking. He also continued thinking. Perhaps Pak Senik wanted his father to join in on some project. If he did, Semaun would be amazed. They had never consulted his father about anything before. Semaun felt that they spent all day and night praying for his father's death. They wanted the family out of Banggul Derdap as well. But the land belonged to his family. It had been carefully entrusted from one generation to the next. The five fields were not only ancestral property; they were the very lifeblood of the whole family. The old house, hidden among the tall coconut trees, belonged to the family. Semaun would not readily give away anything that belonged to his family. He would fight for what was theirs. He would face any challenge. He would rather die than have his father disturbed in any way. He wanted his mother to feel proud of the five plots of land. He wanted Semek to grow and then marry.

The thought of his sister made him turn around.

'What did you say?' he asked.

'I said not to frown like that,' she replied. 'He might have come to help us.'

'Help us?' Semaun shouted, laughing as he did so. 'Did you say he might have come to help us? The Day of Judgement will come before that happens.'

Semek said nothing.

'When has anyone ever offered to help us?' continued Semaun. 'I've never noticed. They hate me too much. They say I'm violent. I'm a tiger. The devil. They'd all like to see us go somewhere else.'

Semek remained silent. Semaun continued walking. Semek followed him.

The sun was high in the sky by the time Semaun and his sister reached their overgrown front yard. The fierce heat stabbed into the tops of their heads. The slush on Semaun's body and legs had begun to dry, forming little clusters here and there, the colour of Thai face-powder. Semaun stopped briefly at the foot of the stairs and slowly took the weed-cutter down from his shoulder.

Its blade shone in the bright sunlight. Semek changed her direction and walked towards the back of the house. Semaun fixed his eyes on the man who was busy yarning with his father on the front verandah. His mother squatted attentively in the doorway.

'Ah, here's Semaun,' Pak Kasa informed his guest.

The guest turned his face towards the stairs. Semaun recognized him at once, Pak Senik, headman of Banggul Derdap village.

'Have you been cutting weeds?' Pak Senik called out.

In reply, Semaun raised his forehead. It was covered with dried splashes of mud.

'Pak Senik wants to talk about the fields,' Pak Kasa said, opening the discussion. 'I don't know anything about it. That's why I sent Semek to get you.'

Semaun sat on the third step.

'What about the fields?' Semaun demanded.

Pak Senik changed his position slightly. He hung his legs over the cross-beam between the verandah and the bamboo platform.

'The village is considering planting two crops a year,' Pak Senik said. He glanced at Pak Kasa and then back at Semaun. Semaun's face was dirty. It was covered with mud. Little patches of dried earth were starting to show on his body and legs as well.

'Well?'

'We'd like everyone to do it.'

'I don't want to.'

Pak Senik was silent. Again he looked at Pak Kasa, wanting his support. Pak Kasa said nothing. Pak Senik turned towards Mak Leha, who was still sitting dumbfounded. Quite clearly, he hoped that the two old creatures who were father and mother to the muddy youth on the stairs would support him. Pak Kasa still said nothing. Mak Leha was also speechless. It was for their son to decide. He looked after them, and had done so since Pak Kasa's cough became serious. Semaun's opinion was the only one that mattered.

'If you don't, none of us will be able to,' Pak Senik explained. 'That's an important condition. We all have to agree on it. If we do, the government will give us fertilizer, a tractor, and irrigation facilities.'

'I don't want to,' Semaun replied.

Pak Kasa was starting to feel restless. He was muttering to himself. He knew what sort of a temper his son had. There would be no stopping him if he got angry. Always quick to take offence, there was a persistent sense of hostility between the villagers and himself which he greatly resented. One wrong movement and Pak Senik would catch a slap across the nose. But the old man wouldn't speak out. He wouldn't have known what to say. He shifted over towards his wife. They whispered something to each other. Mak Leha got up from the doorway and went inside.

'Why not?' Pak Senik resumed.

'I don't want to,' Semaun replied sullenly. He had good reasons for not wanting to get involved, but he couldn't be bothered telling Pak Senik what they were. It was very hot and it wouldn't have taken much to bring him to the boil.

Pak Senik drew his legs in underneath him and sat up straight. It was his way of getting ready to explain something in considerable detail. But as he did so, Semek came down the back stairs. She walked over to her brother and said something to him that Pak Senik couldn't quite hear. Semaun came down the stairs and grabbed his weed-cutter. Then the two of them started out for the river. Pak Senik was caught totally off guard. He had absolutely no idea what was happening. Formally excusing himself, he stood and started down the ladder. Pak Kasa and Mak Leha said nothing. They got to their feet and watched him go.

Once Pak Senik was some distance across the ricefields, Pak Kasa quickly grabbed his cane with the three-branched handle from against the wall and left the house. As he climbed down the stairs, he swung the cane at some clumps of grass beside the path. Mak Leha still said nothing. She knew where her husband was going.

When he reached the river, he found Semaun up to his chest in the water. Each time he bobbed under the surface, small ripples formed. The waves beat against the bank and the ironwood trunk jutting out from it. Semek squatted on the trunk, watching Semaun wash himself. Pak Kasa made his way slowly down to the bathing stage and then squatted beside his completely absorbed daughter.

Instantly, Semaun leapt out of the water and sat on the trunk. The slush had gone from his body, and his heavy, knotted muscles were once again obvious. He raised his hands, displaying his broad, well-proportioned chest.

'Why did you refuse?' his father asked.

'I don't want to.'

'Why not?'

'Lots of reasons,' Semaun replied. 'We can't trample on the customs of our ancestors, even if it would make us four times as rich as before.'

Semaun couldn't possibly agree to the proposal. Pak Senik was greedy. He wanted to make a fortune in a hurry, by dishonest means. Semaun's children would be cursed for the next seven generations if he accepted the scheme. He wouldn't accept it, not by so much as a single grain of rice. He wouldn't trample on the customs of the ancestors. Offending tradition was like spitting in your own parent's face. Insulting your parents was like defiling the graves and souls of your forebears. The man who defiled the traditions of the ancestors would have his backbone broken and his ribs cracked as soon as he was placed in his tomb. Semaun didn't want to suffer in the grave. He didn't want to visit his sins on the other members of his family. He couldn't bear to think of their bones being shattered by the red earth. He wanted to live in peace. He wanted to die in peace.

'Why haven't they ever asked us to share in anything else?' Semaun continued, trying to hide his real motives. 'What's so special about this project? We should have had a cow. Why didn't he want to talk about that? Someone shifted the boundary stone. Why didn't we all meet and talk about that? Why do they treat us like mangy dogs?'

Pak Kasa looked at his son's glistening body. Semek was busy pushing dead leaves away from the side of the trunk with a dye-shrub branch. Pak Kasa did not speak. There was a good deal of truth in what his son said. The villagers avoided them and treated the family as though they were possessed. Pak Kasa had felt that too. He was pretty wild when he was young. He lived only for himself. But that was a long time ago. Why did they still not want him? He was old now. Before long he'd be leaving the damned village forever. He wasn't about to bow his head and ask them to pity him.

'If they want to plant twice a year, they can,' Semaun continued. 'They could plant three or four times a year if they want to. We plant once a year, that's enough. We don't want to torture the land we've inherited. The fields are our soul. Our heart. We were made of earth. We return to the earth. What will happen if we torture the earth, our soul? It will be angry with us. And what if the earth is angry? The rice will fail. The earth will kill us.'

Semaun stopped poking at the leaves and twigs as they swirled past the log. She nodded. Pak Kasa could feel the truth of what Semaun was saying. In fact, he should have been telling his son those things. For some reason or other, he wasn't as aggressive as he used to be. He was old. It was time to get rid of his violent ways. Anyhow, Pak Senik wasn't to blame. The villagers had turned him against the family. He deeply respected the village headman. But he wouldn't give in like a fool over this issue. Pak Kasa added his nod to that of his daughter.

'A man drunk with wealth never really thinks about what he's doing,' Pak Kasa said, once he had stopped nodding in agreement with his children. 'All the barns in the village are brimming with rice and yet they still want more. Dogol has got enough rice in his round bark barn to reach right up to the roof. Jusoh and Lebai Debasa have enough fields for themselves, their children, and their children's children as well. They're the ones who sent Pak Senik here to win us over.'

Semaun leapt back into the water and dived under. The ripples sent the leaves and twigs bouncing away from the log. He lifted his head out of the water, then ducked it under several times. Next he quickly jumped back on the ironwood log. He swung his arms in the air, and shook his head, sending drops of water flying in all directions. Semek wiped a few drops from her forehead.

'Our land is different from other land,' Semaun continued, now that he had settled back onto the log again. 'It has been passed from one generation of our ancestors to the next. It isn't like the main road—you just can't dig it up any time you feel like it.'

Pak Kasa and his daughter listened intently. The old man had never thought of the land as a sacred trust, or how they ought to honour the earth because it sustained them. Such things had never concerned him very much. He felt considerably relieved by Semaun's statements. The earth had fed his ancestors for hundreds of years; he couldn't torture it.

'We mustn't rip the surface of the earth open twice a year,' Semaun said. 'Once a year is proper. Mankind is too arrogant. He never feels compassion for the earth. The earth has its feelings as well. But it can't tell us what they are. Man has to use his mind and decide for himself.'

Semek agreed wholeheartedly with her brother's

explanation. Mankind had changed a lot. People no longer honoured the earth which sustained them and their families. They only wanted to gratify their own desires, in the most selfish way possible. Other people's sufferings never bothered them. The earth suffered, didn't it?

Pak Kasa stood up, followed by Semek. Semaun, still dressed in his wet sarong, joined them on the bank. The three family members walked slowly home together.

'The village rice lands were once forest,' Pak Kasa told them as they climbed the slope beside the river. 'The forest was as thick as the jungle is today. All sorts of wild animals lived there. Tigers. Elephants. Our ancestors cleared that land. They planted it and cared for it, as carefully as they cared for their own children. And now, suddenly, they want to torture it twice each year.'

'The land won't complain,' Semaun chimed in. 'It hasn't got a mouth. There's no way it can cry out for mercy. Human beings have to think for it. We're human. All human beings can think.'

'Pak Senik and his supporters can plant twice a year,' added Semek. 'There's no need for us to. Time will tell which one of us is right.'

No one answered Semek's chatter; neither Pak Kasa, who was walking in front of her, nor Semaun, who was the last in line. But inwardly Semaun agreed completely. As far as he was concerned, he would continue planting once a year. Pak Senik could do whatever he wanted, it made no difference. Semaun didn't mind planting at a different time to the rest of the village. Let them plant twice a year, he couldn't care less.

When they reached their yard, they were surprised to find not only Mak Leha waiting for them, still squatting in the doorway, but Pak Senik as well. The headman hadn't gone home after all, although he had started off across the fields. He wanted a definite answer. Did they support the scheme or not? It was an important question. He wanted to convey the village's decision to the relevant authorities. If Semaun agreed, the whole village would be better off. That was what he had always wanted. But if they absolutely refused to participate, there would be nothing more that Pak Senik could do. Only one path would remain open: he would have to abandon compromise. In future, if Semaun was violent, he would have to be violent too. Force would have to be met with force. There were limits to even Pak Senik's patience. If any one of the villagers wanted to go their own way, to be kings in their heart and sultans in their own eyes, he would be obliged to forget all his patience. Pak Senik would do what had to be done; regardless of whether the defaulter was Semaun or Dogol, his own right-hand man.

Because the three family members were so startled, Mak Leha got up and rushed to the end of the bamboo platform.

'Pak Senik wants to know what we've decided,' the old woman said, shaking as though she'd been possessed by a demon.

Her mother's nervous movements on the raised bamboo platform made Semek act at once. She spun around and grabbed hold of her brother's firm right wrist. She tugged his hand with the same vigour she would have used to pull out a dead coconut tree stump, terrified he might bound up the stairs and hit Pak Senik hard across the nose. Pak Senik was leaning comfortably against a cross-beam. Semek was relieved to find that her gesture had been effective. Semaun started to move; the brother and sister ran around the house and up the kitchen stairs. Even that short time was probably enough to cool her brother's anger.

'Will you do it?' Pak Senik asked briefly.

Pak Kasa climbed the stairs as soon as he realized what Pak Senik was asking. Mak Leha stood on the platform and watched her husband pass.

'Will you do it?' Pak Senik repeated, once Pak Kasa and Mak Leha had sat down on the front verandah.

Gathering his strength, Pak Kasa sighed. He shook his head. 'Everyone else has agreed,' Pak Senik replied, 'including the Tok Imam, and Jusoh, Lebai Debasa and Dogol. Everyone, that is, except one person.'

'Who?' Pak Kasa asked, absent-mindedly.

'You.'

'I won't do it.'

'Why not? Everyone else in the village has agreed.'

'I've got all the rice I need.'

Pak Senik laughed mockingly at Pak Kasa pretending not to be greedy. Mak Leha frowned at her uninvited guest's ridicule.

'I won't torture the land I've received from my ancestors,' continued Pak Kasa. Again Pak Senik laughed. When his laughter had died down, he asked, 'What do you mean "torture the land"?'

'The land needs to rest. You'd be planting all the time. One season after another. The earth couldn't take it. It would make us humans thin too, working hard every day in the fields.'

A smile spread across Pak Senik's lips. That was a funny thing for someone who never had anything to do with any other human beings to say. He wanted to tell Pak Kasa what a fool he was; a comic fool. But if he said what he was thinking, Pak Kasa would get angry. Semaun would jump out. Mak Leha's expression would change to one of intense annoyance. No one could help being angry if they were told that they were even more stupid than a water-buffalo.

'The land is there to be planted,' Pak Senik explained, although he realized that Pak Kasa and his family never really listened to anyone else. 'It doesn't have any other function. It grows rice. Anyway, how would it know if it was being hurt or not? It can't feel anything. It isn't alive.'

Pak Kasa flushed. His heart beat more quickly. Remembering how fierce he used to be in his youth, Pak Kasa wished he could summon up the attitude of the wounded bull buffalo again, but he was too old now. He wanted to tell Pak Senik that people who were eager for material wealth were ignorant and irreligious. His land wasn't like the main highway. All sorts of filth fell on the highway, a thousand and one different varieties of men stamped on it day and night. This was sacred land. Ancestral land. It sustained us all. If there were no rice land, then there would be nothing to eat. And if there were nothing to eat, there would be no one living in Banggul Derdap. The land helped us. We have to help the land. Pak Kasa wanted to shout out what a pagan Pak Senik was. He wanted to tell the village headman that the land was conscious and knew when it was being hurt, although it could not speak. And, further, that we mustn't insult the ancestors. They had planted once a year for centuries. Why should we want to plant twice a year? But he didn't say any of that. He didn't want to fight with Pak Senik in front of his own house. He knew that the real fault didn't lie with Pak Senik.

'I can't agree,' he said simply.

'You can't force people to do things they don't want,' a harsh voice at the doorway suddenly said. They all turned to the direction the voice had come from. Semaun was squatting in the doorway. He stared at Pak Senik's nose. The two men were no more than two armspans apart.

'I can't violate the traditional law,' Pak Kasa said quickly, as though trying to stop Pak Senik from answering his son's words. There was every likelihood that Semaun would attack Pak Senik if he said the wrong thing. Pak Kasa didn't want his verandah turned into a cockpit, even if one of the antagonists was Semaun, his

only son and the family's sole support.
'We can't violate tradition,' Semaun repeated. He stepped over the threshold and tightened the knot in the centre of his sarong. Although he considered Semaun's idea of traditional customary law ludicrous, Pak Senik did not dare laugh.
'Which tradition?' he insisted softly.
'Our ancestors' tradition,' Semaun replied roughly.
'They were ignorant. They weren't interested in what anyone else had to say. Their day has passed. So has the day of the white man. We're an independent nation now. We're self-governing. And we have to be self-supporting as well.'
Mak Leha felt extremely uneasy. Semek pressed her face closer to the door. Pak Senik was making a dangerous mistake in talking to Semaun like that. Pak Kasa muttered quietly to himself.
'We don't want to torture the ancestral earth,' Semaun snarled. 'You're a fool, Pak Senik!'
'How can anyone torture the earth?' Pak Senik replied. 'The earth gives us life, that's all. If we plant twice a year, the earth will be able to help us twice as much. We'll be doing the earth a favour. It will be delighted. It would be even more delighted if we could plant three times a year.'
'I won't do it,' Pak Kasa said decisively. 'I don't care if everybody else does, but I won't violate traditional law.'
Pak Senik was dumb. He could feel his hopes collapsing around him. His wish to bring the villagers to the path of prosperity had been completely thwarted. It was even more galling to hear the outdated arguments which had been raised against the project. Some men were absolute idiots and would oppose anything. Pak Senik remembered how Jusoh and Lebai Debasa had insisted that he ought to use force against Semaun, because Semaun made such a nuisance of himself around Dunggul

Derdap. Pak Senik's patience was at an end; there was nothing to be gained from further compromise. He would take action the next time Semaun did something which disturbed the peace of the village.

'Get out of here!' shouted Semaun.

Pak Senik was stunned. He floundered about like a lost man on a dark night. When he looked at Pak Kasa, the old man's eyes glared back at him, five times as fiercely as before. Pak Senik turned and looked at Mak Leha, seemingly pleading for her pity. Mak Leha said nothing. There was an oppressive silence. Nothing like this had ever happened to him before. He was being chased away like a dog.

'Get out!' Semaun repeated, slapping his hands against his thighs.

Pak Senik made his way very slowly to the edge of the platform. He didn't jump up and run for his life, like a child frightened of the bogey-man. In fact, he wasn't at all frightened. He was distressed to hear a boy from his own village chasing him away as if he was a mangy dog. Had anyone else besides that worthless family been there, he would have felt deeply humiliated. Although he wanted to spin around and fight the wounded bull of a youth, he realized how stupid that would be. It would take more than a set of knuckles to stop the violence in the world nowadays. People like Semaun would learn their lesson one day, Pak Senik thought, but not by fighting. When the village started to progress, Semaun's rebellious spirit would be broken in a far more subtle way. Pak Senik was prepared to wait for that happy day to come. He could wait. As long as God was prepared to grant him a little extra time. Feeling no better than a scabby dog driven off with a cold piece of firewood, Pak Senik left. Turning neither to right nor left, he walked straight away from the solitary house. On reaching the rice-fields, he stopped. A few tears had formed in the corners of his eyes and he wiped them

The Wounded Bull

away with the end of his jacket. He lamented the stupidity of one of his villagers.

Pak Senik started walking along the still bare dividing wall. There would be no going back this time. Nothing could be gained from talking to fools like Pak Kasa and his son Semaun.

Midday had passed. The fields were full of water. Once they'd been drained, the villagers could start harrowing the ground. When they had finished, the women would gather the young shoots. Then, before long, the rice would start to grow. Pak Senik suspected that this was probably the last time that the fields in his village would be planted only once a year. He would continue to work towards double planting, even though one family, Pak Kasa's family, objected. Pak Kasa's family could follow the seasons, if they wanted. They would be the only ones doing so.

Pak Senik kept walking. When he reached the corner of the fields near Jusoh's house, he thought of going to tell him the results of the discussion with Semaun, but then decided the time was wrong. Jusoh would be stretched out, resting after a hard day's work in the open air. Anyway, there wasn't really anything to discuss. There was no place in the village community for Pak Kasa.

Once the rice had been harvested this year, the tractors could go straight into the fields and rip the weeds out. That seemed reasonable. They could gradually pump water from the river. Pak Senik imagined the lush, Taiwanese grain. He could see the villagers in their fields, shouting for joy. Their happiness would be his. He wondered how Semaun and Pak Kasa would react. Their fields would be dry and empty. Pak Senik wouldn't actually do anything. He just wanted to watch. He wanted to see Pak Kasa and Semaun's faces, after they had almost killed themselves looking after their beloved ancestors.

3
Day into Night

Semaun felt very apprehensive as he made his way down to his fields that particular morning. His father had coughed all night. And, often, not only coughed but vomited blood as well. Semaun had several times boiled various medicinal herbs together, but the old man continued to vomit and spit blood. Sometimes he terrified the family by bringing up hard, congealed lumps. Semek and her mother continually massaged his chest. On one occasion, he had coughed up an enormous amount. There was almost half a cup of solid blood. Semek wept as she went to the window to tip the half-cupful of blood out. Towards dawn, his coughing had eased a little. Semaun had waited for the roosters to crow before starting out from home. There was still one plot left to be weeded.

He worried about Dogol too. Dogol wanted to destroy him. Semaun felt as though he would like to cut Dogol's head off. But the thought of his sister, who was still growing up, his mother, and his sick father, made him restrain himself. He didn't want to think of what could happen to his family if he wasn't there. They would be more vulnerable on their own. He remembered how Lebai Debasa and Jusoh had rushed him, trying to provoke a fight a few years ago. Semaun knew the different ways the villagers had schemed to get his family off their ancestral land. His ancestors had lived in Banggul

Derdap as long as anyone else; the village was as much his as it was theirs. He wouldn't let a few passing strangers disturb the land of his ancestors.

He swung his weed-cutter rhythmically. Each time the blade of the scythe smacked against the water, the rushes broke. Some of the leaves flew high up into the air.

This was the last field. Semaun expected to finish weeding that same morning. In the evening he would drain off the water, so that the roots could rot. It wouldn't take more than a couple of days to remove the water. Then he would start turning the soil. He should finish that in four or five days. Semek had collected the young shoots and tied them in bundles. The bundles lay on the dividing walls, ready to be replanted. Semaun's mind moved from the bundles of rice-shoots to Pak Senik, the village headman, and the two visits Pak Senik had paid his family. Semaun stopped swinging the weed-cutter. Fixing the implement firmly in the ground, he waded slowly through the water to the dividing walls and then sat down. Although the walls had not fully hardened, small blades of grass were already starting to show through. Had it not been for Pak Senik, his family would probably have been kicked out of the village a long time ago. Had it not been for him, their house could well have been attacked by a mob of villagers. Semaun could see how Pak Senik had stood by the family on various occasions. He regretted the harsh way he had treated the old man when he came to discuss double planting. Sincerely and fully regretted it. He wanted to get up and go to Pak Senik's house to tell him so. Suddenly he heard someone shouting: it was Semek, his sister. Semaun turned around. He could see her in the distance, running across the walls towards him. Anxiously he waited for her to arrive. She had never run so fast across the rice-fields before. Something serious must have happened at home. Perhaps their father had started coughing again. Or someone had come and was making trouble.

'Brother! Brother!' she panted loudly.

Semaun frowned.

'Brother! Brother!'

When she reached him, she was panting. He could tell how exhausted she was from the expression on her face and the quick rise and fall of her breast.

'Is it Pak Senik?'

She did not reply. She was breathing too quickly to be able to speak yet. Instead, she shook her head. Semaun took hold of her soft shoulders and shook her. She flopped backwards and forwards as though the life had gone out of her.

'Is it Dogol?'

Again she shook her head.

'Has something happened to father?'

She nodded.

'What?'

Semek could scarcely speak.

'He. . . .' She couldn't go on. Pressing her wet face against her brother's muddy chest, Semek started to howl.

Almost disdainfully, Semaun pushed the girl aside, and started to run home along the embankments, leaving his weed-cutter standing aggressively in the middle of the field. Although she had not yet caught her breath, Semek started to follow him once she realized what he was doing. She was still crying.

'Brother! Brother!'

Semaun heard her shout but ignored her completely. He didn't even turn around. He was concentrating on his father. The old man had coughed all night. Was he dead? It was a terrifying thought. The villagers had hated him for years. What would they do once he dies? How would they treat the family in the future?

Semaun quickened his pace, still closely followed by

Semek. On reaching the stairs, he rushed straight inside. His mother lay on the floor, beside his father who was stretched out on a sleeping mat. Semaun took his father's limp wrist, trying to find out if the old man's pulse was still beating. He was relieved to discover that it was. Semek had taken her place beside her mother. She was exhausted. He turned towards her.

'He was having trouble breathing,' said the girl. 'We were both worried about him.'

'He's still alive,' Semaun replied.

'I didn't say he wasn't,' Semek told him. 'He was having trouble breathing.'

Semaun turned around towards his father again. Mak Leha raised her head and stared at the prone body of her husband. Semaun tried his father's wrist once more, then placed his hand on the old man's thin chest. He rubbed his father's chest several times.

'Father! Father!'

There was no obvious reply. Semaun turned to his mother and sister. 'Get me some medicinal oil, please.'

'Mother's already massaged him a lot.'

Semaun had run out of ideas. Medicinal oil was all he could think of. Perhaps a few herbal mixtures as well, but nothing more. And he had already used them last night.

'We ought to call a *bomoh*,' his mother suddenly suggested.

Startled, Semaun turned towards his mother. He did not say a word. After staring intently at her, he turned and looked at Semek, who was squatting beside her. There was an expression of despair on the girl's face.

'Call the *bomoh* from Balek Bukit village,' his mother repeated. 'Or the Imam.'

Semaun was still stunned. He couldn't imagine going out and pleading with the villagers for help. That damned Dogol had turned them all against him. So had Jusoh and Lebai Debasa. There would be no point in it. He knew what people thought of him and his family. He would rather his father died without him trying to get the *bomoh*.

'What are you waiting for?' his mother insisted. 'You go, Semek.'

Semek shivered. She looked at her father's weary face; then at her brother and her mother. Disappointment showed in both their faces. It was as though Mak Leha had suddenly realized why her children were reluctant to go. She knew the insults the villagers had hurled at all of them over the years. The old woman stared at her children's troubled expressions. A few tears rolled down her face and onto her lap. When she saw the tears falling from her mother's eyes, Semek bowed and pressed her own pale face into the old woman's lap. Mak Leha put her hand on the back of her daughter's neck, and stroked the girl's thick hair. The trickle of tears suddenly became a torrent. Semaun felt choked. His eyes reflected his confusion. Of course he fought back when anybody abused him. He could be as gentle as the next person given the chance, but he wouldn't stand by and see his family hurt and disappointed. He'd cut off three finger-joints first. A gentle response to violence only invited further, harsher violence. The most effective counter was violence itself. It wasn't really clear why the villagers were so antagonistic towards himself and his family. He wanted to live like everyone else. Semaun remembered Dogol, and tried to think if he had ever done anything wrong to him. His mind was blank. He'd never deliberately set out to be cruel to Dogol. Or to anyone else, for that matter.

And now his father was dying. Semaun would feel even more unwanted and lonely without his father.

'But we never did anything to hurt them.'

The words came out so easily that Semaun was as startled as Semek and Mak Leha. His mother lifted her head as though it had been someone else speaking, then

turned and looked at her daughter. Semek was still crying.
'What did we do?' Mak Leha asked.
Semaun regained control of himself. He looked into his mother's eyes.
'When did we ever hurt them?'
Semaun did not answer.
'Your father, you mean?'
Semek, too, was startled.
'It happened a long time ago,' their mother continued. 'A long time ago. Your father went on a rampage. People were doing things to upset us. They couldn't bear to see us happy and living in peace. They were jealous. They accused your father of hamstringing their cows. They accused him of knocking holes in their irrigation channels. They accused him of stealing grass. They accused him of letting the water out of their fish-ponds. They accused him of all sorts of things. He was sentenced. Punished, just like that. All because a few people in Banggul Derdap couldn't bear to see anyone else better off than themselves. They were just like animals.'
As she finished, Pak Kasa's lips started to move.
'He wants some water,' Semaun called out.
Semek offered a dish of boiled herbal mixture and a newly-picked betel-leaf. Pouring the medicine onto the leaf, Semaun let the drops fall into his father's mouth. Pak Kasa was still muttering. Semaun gave the dish back to Semek, then stood up.
'Where are you going?' his mother asked anxiously.
'To Pak Senik.'
'To his house?'
Semaun nodded.
'Why?'
'I have to go. He'll come, I know he will.'
'But. . . .'
'But what?' he asked softly.

His mother made no reply.

'We just can't leave Father like this. At least we can get him ready. There needs to be someone who can help send him on his way. If Pak Senik comes and reads verses from the Quran, that'll be enough. We won't feel so bad then either. We ought to do what we can.'

'But Pak Senik hates us. He wants us to plant twice a year. He wants to drive us out of the village.'

Semaun squatted beside his mother and took hold of her hand.

'No, he doesn't. He's not as fierce as we think he is. I shouldn't have been so rude to him the other day. He's a good man. We'd have been driven out a long time ago if it hadn't been for him.'

'But. . . .'

'He isn't a violent man. The others have made him like that. Just as they made father and me violent. They want him to get rid of us. They're using him.'

'Who is?' she demanded.

'Dogol.'

'Dogol?'

Semaun nodded.

'Dogol said your father crippled his cow. Is he the one that's accusing you too?'

Semaun nodded again.

'Who else?'

'Lebai Debasa, I guess.'

'Why?'

'He's always with Dogol.'

'And who else?'

'Jusoh, probably.'

His mother nodded, then asked, 'Siti's man, Jusoh?'

Semaun nodded.

'They not only want to get rid of us; they're trying to find a way of getting rid of Pak Senik as well.'

'Pak Senik's an old man, isn't he?'

'That's why they want to get rid of him.'

Without stopping to wash the mud from his body or change his wet sarong, Semaun leapt down the stairs and began hurrying towards the village headman's house. He took the most direct path, through the rice-fields. As he rushed along the dividing walls, his foot sometimes slipped off the embankment into the mud, but he paid no attention and kept on running. All his hopes were fixed on the headman. Pak Senik wasn't a *bomoh*, but Semaun knew that he would do whatever he could for them. At least he would try to help Pak Kasa regain consciousness. Semaun seemed completely dependent on Pak Senik now. Whether his father lived or died was something only God could decide. Semaun would never forget any assistance the headman could offer. When things returned to normal, Semaun would try to explain to the headman why he had been so wild over the years. He would tell Pak Senik why he had been so aggressive the last few months. Semaun and his family could think about double planting again.

Semaun continued running, helter-skelter across the fields. The villagers were still cutting weeds. As he passed, some of them jerked their heads up quickly, like a frightened water-buffalo. When they realized it was Semaun, they returned to their task. Semaun must have gone mad at last. Perhaps he thought there was something chasing him. Semaun ignored them. He was preoccupied with his family's problems and with Pak Senik.

On reaching the house, Semaun stood outside and bellowed Pak Senik's name. Pak Senik looked out of the window. When he saw Semaun standing there, covered in mud, the headman moved swiftly back inside again. Pak Senik feared the worst. His eyes shone wildly as he searched for his machette. Perhaps Semaun's reasons for coming were as foul as the rest of him. As he opened the door, the headman slipped his machette against the wall.

'Pak Senik! Pak Senik!'

Pak Senik heard him but did not reply. He listened and waited for Semaun to come to the bottom of the stairs.

'Pak Senik! Pak Senik!'

Pak Senik stood in the doorway. Only when Semaun reached the stairs, did he cross the threshold and walk out onto the wooden structure.

'What do you want?'

Semaun swayed as he tried to catch his breath.

'You haven't been annoying the other villagers again, have you?'

Semaun shook his head. He made no reply. The other villagers were of no concern to him. His father was dangerously ill. Death could take him at any moment. He was only interested in talking about his father.

'What do you want?'

'My father is dangerously ill,' Semaun said briefly.

'What's wrong with him?'

'He coughed all last night. He could scarcely breathe.'

'Have you called Pak Busu?'

Semaun shook his head.

'Who's with him now?'

'Just my mother and my sister.'

Pak Senik paused. He knew what the other villagers thought of the family. Then he went inside, took his shawl and his walking stick, and came outside again. Semaun led the way. Pak Senik followed him. When they reached the same path Semaun had followed across the rice-fields, the headman suddenly called out, 'Where are you going?'

Semaun was startled.

'Let's go to Pak Busu's house first. Perhaps he can fix us some medicine.'

And Pak Senik immediately turned left, to follow the track along the edge of the rice land. Semaun stopped briefly, then hurried to catch up with him.

As they walked, Semaun seemed to be struggling to say something, but was unable to get the words out. He was worried that the villagers might want to drive Pak Senik's family away as well as his own, if the headman helped them. But the fear remained bottled up inside himself. It was for God to decide. Semaun honestly believed that God was on his side.

They passed a few villagers gossiping in the middle of the track. The villagers looked at them, amazed, then moved to let them pass, before whispering to each other. None of them greeted Pak Senik, let alone Semaun. They had given him up a long time ago, for no very good reason.

'I'm sorry,' Semaun suddenly said.

On hearing Semaun's voice, Pak Senik almost stopped. He checked himself and kept walking.

'Sorry for what?' he asked, surprised.

'For the way I spoke to you the other day.'

'When?' Pak Senik pretended to have forgotten the shameful incident.

'At our house.'

Their conversation suddenly lapsed. They had reached Pak Busu's yard.

'Busu! Busu!' called Pak Senik.

There was no reply, despite the door being wide open. Inside the house, a floorboard banged. Pak Senik looked at Semaun. Semaun deliberately said nothing.

'Busu! Busu!' Pak Senik shouted for the last time. He had expected this the whole way. Semaun wasn't the sort of person who was worth helping. He was a giant stinging-nettle, as far as Banggul Derdap village was concerned. Everyone in the district was prepared to believe the worst about him.

Pak Senik made no comment. They went, leaving the *bomoh* hiding in his own house. The headman had no further questions to put to Semaun. Too many things were turning around in his mind. Pak Busu was an absolute heathen. Pak Senik thought of Dogol's proposals to have Semaun and his family driven out of the village. He recalled Jusoh and Lebai Debasa fully supported the demands. Even the Imam from the religious school wanted Semaun and his family kicked out of Banggul Derdap. There was something fishy about Dogol's proposals. Pak Senik was starting to get suspicious. But the villagers weren't as stupid as they used to be. They were starting to think for themselves. Their eyes were open now. One day, even Pak Busu would be able to tell what was true and what was not.

'Do you know where Dogol has gone?' Pak Senik asked as they sped along.

Semaun did not reply. He was too busy thinking about his father lying at home.

'He's gone away. So has his wife. The place is deserted.'

The answer stunned Semaun. He was amazed Pak Senik showed so little concern. It was dangerous to let Dogol do as he pleased. He was probably up to no good. Where was he? At the house of his parents-in-law, perhaps. But he hadn't finished his fields yet. Nor had he made any arrangements about his house or the land around it. Dogol wasn't too far away. He'd be back soon. There'd be no mistaking it when he came. Semaun wondered whether Pak Senik knew something he wasn't telling him. He also wanted to ask about Jusoh and Lebai Debasa. Perhaps they were planning to do something wrong. There wasn't time to inquire; they had just about reached the house. Semaun led Pak Senik in through the gate. Ahead of them, Mak Leha stood in the doorway, wiping an occasional tear from her eyes.

'Please come up,' she greeted him.

Pak Senik nodded and immediately climbed the wooden stairs. The house was oppressively silent. It was also very untidy. There was no one inside, apart from Pak Kasa and his daughter. Semek moved politely away from her father's side and towards the wall, to make room for Pak Senik. Pak Senik thanked her with a nod, then moved to Pak Kasa's side. Semaun had gone down to the river to wash the mud off himself.

Pak Senik very slowly lifted one of the old man's eyelids. The whites of his eyes had gone yellow, and the tangled veins were easily discernible. Pak Senik then put his hand on Pak Kasa's chest, trying to establish his heartbeat. Two pairs of eyes watched him closely. They were joined by another set of eyes. Semaun had finished washing.

Semaun trusted Pak Senik completely. He would do whatever the headman wanted. If he asked for a coconut shell of water and a plate of parched rice, Semaun would send his sister off to get them at once. He knew the headman would do everything possible. Pak Senik would try to get the old man to open his mouth and take a spoonful of rice. He would try to stop the old man coughing. They waited for Pak Senik to do something. For a long time, Pak Senik simply massaged the old man's chest. The village leader's lips moved as though he was imploring the assistance of the Almighty. Suddenly a few tears fell on Pak Kasa's prone chest. The tears came from Pak Senik's chin. Semek whispered something to her brother. Semaun nodded. She slowly wiped the tears from her eyes.

'Pak Senik!' she whispered softly.

Pak Senik turned around; he was crying. 'Please fetch me a Quran,' he asked.

Sobbing, Semek immediately rushed to her father's side. She took his hand and held it tightly against her cheek. Mak Leha didn't know what to do. She shuffled along the floor, then started to caress her husband's forehead. The room filled with the pitiful sound of their weeping. Semaun tried to control himself. Wiping his eyes, he jumped up and took a tattered old Quran from a small shelf. He gave it to Pak Senik, then sat near his father's head. No one said a word, although they were all aware how critical the situation was. They each stared at the old man's face as he lay on the floor.

A few moments later, a harsh, broken voice emerged from Pak Senik's mouth. At times, he stopped chanting altogether. Whenever he did, the family wept more loudly. Pak Senik continued chanting. Suddenly he stopped. He edged slightly forward and took hold of Pak Kasa's wrist, pressing his little finger against the artery. Then he looked at Semaun, Semek and Mak Leha. Lifting the cloth from Pak Kasa's stomach, he covered the man's face. On seeing this, Semek screamed, as though possessed by a spirit, and buried her face in her mother's lap. Semaun, thoroughly unbalanced by the situation, rushed forward and raised the cloth slightly from his father's face. He kissed the old man's pale face.

'He's gone,' Pak Senik whispered, as they sobbed.

No one replied.

'Do you want to bury him today?' Pak Senik continued, once he was sure that no one intended replying to his previous remark.

Semaun looked at his mother.

She nodded.

'Wood?'

Semaun looked at his mother.

'Do you want a wooden coffin?' Pak Senik repeated.

'It doesn't matter,' Mak Leha replied, stroking her daughter's hair. 'A plain white shroud will do.'

She took a red, ten dollar bill out of the purse she carried at her waist and offered it to Pak Senik.

'Please make the necessary arrangements for us.'

Pak Senik turned to Semaun, then took the red banknote. He left the house and disappeared down the road. Semaun's mother watched him go, confident he would arrange the funeral properly. Semaun stood up and went to another part of the house to find something. He returned with a saw. Holding the tool in his hand, he walked under the house to find some planks of wood which he could cut into six-foot lengths to line the grave. Semek and her mother remained beside the corpse. From time to time, they lifted the cloth. Every time Mak Leha's eyes met the pale face of the corpse, she started to howl again and dropped the piece of batik material.

'Semaun!' she called.

When she got no response, she stood up, crossed the threshold, and went down to the ground to find her son. Semek watched her, with sad, dulled eyes.

Semaun was still struggling with the wooden boards. He was vigorously sawing one piece after another. His mother stood behind him, without him realizing. She stared intently at his sweaty back, and the heavy muscles in his shoulders and hands. The saw was gripped firmly in his fists. She simply watched him, not saying another word. She wanted to be with her son. No one else would come and help them in any way. Mak Leha knew how isolated the family had always been. She took a step forward.

'Semaun!' she called.

Semaun stopped sawing and turned around. He was confronted with his mother's red eyes. Neither person spoke. Semek was standing further back, up on the bamboo platform. They all looked at each other. After a long period, Semaun turned back to the wood and started sawing again.

On seeing her son return to his work, Mak Leha turned away. She stopped briefly when she realized her daughter was standing behind her, and looked at the girl. But not for long. Her gaze shifted back to the path. Soon Pak Senik would return, with several yards of white cloth. The lining boards would be finished by then. Two layers of material around the corpse ought to be enough, she thought to herself. Mak Leha walked back up into the house. Semek was again beside the body. Tears streamed from her eyes.

Pak Senik returned with a roll of cloth under his arm. His wife and children were with him. Semaun came out from under the house and stood in the middle of the yard. His mother came to the door. They watched Pak Senik and his family approach. They waited to hear what he had to say. The arrangements for the funeral were entirely in his kind hands.

'I've asked some men to dig the grave,' he called out. 'It cost seven dollars and fifty cents.'

Semaun felt considerably relieved to hear that. Ever since he had gone under the house, he had been wondering who would dig the grave, although he hadn't dared mention it to his mother. It had worried him a lot, but now the problem was solved. He looked at his mother. She opened her purse, took out another red note, and passed it to Semaun. Semaun took the note and offered it to Pak Senik.

'I've already paid for it,' said Pak Senik. 'My tribute to Pak Kasa.'

Semaun was deeply moved. Even though he knew he ought to have thanked the headman, he couldn't. He couldn't speak at all. He gave the money back to his mother. She took the money and put it in her purse again.

'Thank you,' she said, looking at Pak Senik.

The village headman simply nodded.

Again Semaun was deeply moved. He should have thanked Pak Senik. For some reason, he couldn't get the words out. He thought of the harsh words he had hurled so readily at Pak Senik only a few days again. Yet here Pak Senik was doing everything he could to help them. Semaun felt extremely guilty. He resolved he would repay the village headman's kindness.

Pak Senik led his family up the wooden stairs. He didn't really need to be thanked; their faces clearly showed their deep gratitude. He led his family into the house. They sat beside the dead man.

'We'll bury him at five,' Pak Senik said as he started tearing the shroud into the appropriate lengths. Semaun looked uneasy. But Pak Senik soon put his doubts at ease.

'I've asked the men digging the grave to help carry the corpse,' Pak Senik said, measuring the cloth with his hand. 'We will follow it. Do you feel up to coming?' he asked, looking at Mak Leha.

She nodded. Pak Senik turned to Semaun. Semaun stood where he was, dazed.

By half past four, all the preparations were complete. Semek set out a pot of hot coffee and some bread. They waited for the men Pak Senik had employed to come. The sooner they came the better. It wasn't right to keep the body unburied too long. All the family was here. Semaun didn't like to leave the body wrapped in its shroud any longer than was necessary either. Once it had been placed in the grave, it could face the judgement of the angels. He was sure his father was ready for them. Pak Kasa hadn't sinned the way people said he had. His wildness had not been motivated by malice. Society had forced him to go on the rampage.

They waited until half past five. The sun was reddening in the west. Soon it would set. Semaun started to look uncomfortable again. It would be dark in a few hours. He started to fret. Pak Senik got up and walked outside. He looked along the road. There was nothing there. The drum that accompanied the martial arts began playing at the far end of the village. Now and then the drumming gave way to the loud laughter of the young men, who seemed to have no concern for the terrible thing that had happened. Pak Senik tried not to listen to the drumming. No one had a grain of respect for Pak Kasa's body. He ran back inside again. It was almost six o'clock. Twilight was near. In another hour, the caretaker of the mosque would start beating his drum for the early evening prayers. The two families were becoming increasingly restless.

'We can pray here for his soul,' Pak Senik suggested.

Semaun looked around the room, then went to the kitchen to get sufficient water for the purificatory prayers. When he returned, however, the two grave-diggers were standing in the yard.

'Where's the body?' one of them called out in the same tone he would have used to inquire about a stack of chairs at a public entertainment.

Semaun's blood pounded. The grave-digger's coarseness showed how little respect he had for Pak Kasa's remains. Semaun felt strongly tempted to grab his knife and chase the two men away. If no one else wanted to take the body to the graveside, he'd do it himself. Pak Senik took hold of Semaun and tried to calm him.

'We're going to pray for the deceased,' Pak Senik called out to the two men. 'Would you like to join us?'

'Go right ahead,' one of them replied firmly.

Pak Senik didn't want to start an argument, for fear of what the men might do if they were antagonized. The sling was too heavy for him to carry with Semaun. The only other alternative would have been to have Semaun carry the body across his shoulder. Pak Senik led the mourners through the prayers. The rest was up to Semaun. Semek watched her brother from the kitchen. She felt their future would be a little easier now that Pak Senik was prepared to help them, but her father's death was still an enormous loss. She wondered how the villagers would respond to them after this. There were times when Semek was sickened by their mean, petty, vicious behaviour. They were always quarrelling. They hated to see anybody else happy, and would do all they could do to destroy that happiness.

Semek's thoughts were suddenly interrupted; Semaun was calling her.

It was time to put the body onto the sling. Semek

and her brother took Pak Kasa's head and body, Mak Leha took his feet. They slowly carried the body outside. The grave-diggers waited for them at the stairs. They grabbed the body as soon as it arrived. Pak Senik and Semaun took the top end of the sling. The procession began, with Semaun's mother, Semek and Pak Senik's family following at the rear. Soon it would be time for the evening prayer hour. Then day would give way to pitch black night, as black as the life of Semaun and his family without Pak Kasa.

4
Burn! Burn!

Even though Dogol arrived back very late at night, he was up before the sun rose the next morning. He was eager to get to Pak Senik's house and find out what had happened when the headman met Semaun. Obviously the meeting would have been a failure. But Dogol wanted to know how Semaun had reacted. What reasons had he insisted on for not wanting to plant twice a year? Dogol wondered whether Semaun would continue to be as violent, now that Pak Kasa was dead. He hoped so. If Semaun did continue to give Pak Senik a rough time, the old man would have to change his methods. There was no point in discussing things with Semaun. The only thing to do was to have him arrested and thrown in jail. If he couldn't be sentenced, then he ought to be thrown out of the village. Dogol did not realize that strong bonds had been formed between Semaun and Pak Senik. Semaun would never forget Pak Senik's extraordinary kindness until the day he dies.

When Dogol stepped out of his house and looked at the hills, he found that it was still night. The monkeys were still chattering to each other in the forest. It was too early to visit anyone. He leaped down to the ground and slowly made his way to his cow-stall. As he watched the cows enjoying themselves in their own excreta, he thought of Semaun again. Semaun had asked several times for one of the government cows, but Dogol had always refused him, on the grounds that he was a troublemaker. It wasn't a very good reason but the other villagers had accepted it readily enough. The government had given the village fifteen cows. Pak Senik had asked Dogol to distribute them. Dogol now owned two fat cows. Both of them had given birth to bull calves. And now they were pregnant again. Dogol hoped the new calves would be females. He could earn a lot of money if they were.

Dogol kicked the two cows in the back. The cows swished their tails at him, then stood up. One of them flicked its ears forwards as well. Dogol untied them, and without wasting any further time, dragged the two animals out of the stall. The cows walked very slowly, with their big bellies swaying beneath them. Dogol sniggered at their enormous stomachs. The bellies would shower their blessings in a few months.

I'll take the cows to the edge of the swamp, Dogol thought to himself. The grass is very thick. No animals ever graze there. The two bulls frisked along behind. He had not yet fitted them with nose-rings.

By the time he reached the end of the overgrown trail, the sun had risen. Dogol decided to stake the two cows, and then, on his way home, to visit Pak Senik and discuss the current situation.

The track was more and more overgrown as he approached the edge of the swamp. The grass was longer. The moist dew drops wet the end of his sarong and Dogol quickly gathered it around his knees.

When he reached the open space, he drove the stakes into the ground and then stamped on them with his heel, until they were no longer visible. As he stamped, his eyes rapidly surveyed the nearby jungle. His ears caught all sorts of noises. There were dozens of monkeys moving about in the branches of the large trees. Not having eaten since last night, the cows greedily rushed at the lush, damp grass.

After sinking the stakes, Dogol patted one of the cows on the belly. And with that, he turned and started off for Pak Senik's house. Unknown to Dogol, there was a fierce tiger in the noisy jungle. The tiger had not tasted flesh for some considerable time.

Dogol took the most direct route to the headman's house: the red clay road, which had been dug and shaped by endlessly roaring machines. He carried a branch in his hand, and as he walked slowly along, he slashed at the grass by the roadside. Dew flew in all directions. A few mantises leapt out of their hiding places to save themselves.

Dogol kept walking. The road had not yet been finished. It was still uneven; large lumps of clay rose like anthills. Some had fallen over and lay flat like elephant's footprints. Two months ago, work on the road, which was supposed to by-pass the village, had come to a sudden stop. No one knew why. Not even Pak Senik, who should have been told by the District Officer. Nevertheless, most villagers had some explanation to offer. Semaun, son of the recently deceased Pak Kasa, featured in most of them. Dogol blamed Semaun too, and had said so without thinking very much about it. He remembered the afternoon well. Semaun had run amok with a long-bladed machette. The Tamil labourers, who were flattening the road, ran for their lives. The supervisor, leapt up from where he was leaning comfortably against a tree stump, and jumped on his bicycle. There was a tremendous uproar. Everyone wanted to know what had happened. Virtually all of them blamed Semaun, except Pak Senik. He didn't think the fault was one hundred per cent Semaun's. The other party were also to blame. They had started cutting down one of Semaun's largest coconut trees, without telling him beforehand. Pak Senik sometimes suspected that the government of the country was in the hands of uncouth idiots.

Dogol quickly dropped this train of thought as he entered Pak Senik's forked gateway. He threw the branch in his hand away into the undergrowth. He had been using the branch to beat the leeches out of the long grass; it wouldn't be wise to take it into someone's house—especially so early in the day.

The house was still shut up, but someone was in the kitchen. He could see smoke coming out through the wattled roof and spreading in the air. Dogol approached the front stairs, craning his neck to see if there were any signs of Pak Senik being in the front part of the house. There weren't.

'Is the master home?' he called out loudly. His lips broke into a sheepish grin, as though he was aware that his early visit would surely disturb the family.

'Is the master home?' he repeated.

The door between the front portion of the house and the central portion flew open. It sounded like the wind passing through a clump of bamboo. Pak Senik put his head out; then stepped out, across the threshold, hastily pulling his sarong up around his waist. There were seven rolls of flesh under his stout stomach.

'Welcome, welcome,' Pak Senik greeted him politely. 'Dolah, bring some rice out. A plate for me and a plate for Pak Dogol.'

'It looks as though I'm off to a good start,' Dogol said to himself as he washed his feet. He rubbed his legs together, like a man sharpening a knife. The red clay fell away from his ankles and between his toes. He walked across the bamboo platform and into the front part of the house, then sat down carefully.

'Where have you been? I haven't seen you for a while,' Pak Senik asked, scratching his armpit with a piece of bamboo.

'I took my wife to her parents' house.'

'Why?'

'You know what women are like. She couldn't stop

thinking about them.'

Pak Senik smiled.

'What are you doing up so early in the morning?'

'I've been tethering my cows.'

'Where?'

'At the edge of the swamp. The grass is very tall there. I don't think cattle have ever touched it.'

Pak Senik did not reply or asked any further questions. The mention of the untouched long grass reminded him that he had heard a tiger roaring a few nights ago. Father Stripes was probably cooped up somewhere in the undergrowth waiting for a feed. But Pak Senik still said nothing. He was thinking of Pak Kasa. Although he wanted to tell Dogol of the old man's death, for some reason he couldn't.

Dogol must have been talking of the government cows, Pak Senik thought to himself. It was better not to ask; there had almost been a fight over the cows when they first arrived. He knew the source of the disagreement. Dogol hadn't divided the cows among the villagers fairly. Pak Senik knew that. He couldn't remember why he had asked Dogol to do the job. Dogol had justified his not giving one to Semaun by saying that the boy was a troublemaker. Pak Senik felt very guilty about that; everyone should have been treated the same. And that meant Dogol, here now with him, and Semaun, who had long been considered the marauding civet-cat of the village. Pak Senik hadn't chosen to disagree with Dogol over the cows; he was responsible for Dogol. Nor had he wanted to expel Semaun from the village, even though many villagers demanded that he do so; he was equally responsible for Semaun. He had known Semaun from the time he was a child. He had been a wild lad, but that had not been his fault. The others had made him that way. Anger was a disease; it could be cured. And he, Pak Senik, could cure Semaun. He decided that he ought to tell Dogol about Pak Kasa's death. The news might change Dogol's attitude to Semaun. As an older man, Dogol might want to express some sympathy for Semaun. That would influence the other villagers, particularly Jusoh and Lebai Debasa. But it was a hard thing to ask. Dogol would probably not be affected by Pak Kasa's death.

'Is either of them pregnant?' Pak Senik asked, deciding not to say anything for the moment about Pak Kasa.

Dogol nodded. They were both pregnant. He expected them to drop in a few months. Females this time, Dogol thought. He really wanted females. The females could produce more calves. And the calves, if they were females, could have more calves.

'How are the other cows?'

'A lot of them have calved. Some males, some females. All except for Jusoh's beast.'

'Why's that?'

'I guess she's sterile.'

They both smiled at the similarity between Jusoh's cow and his wife. Jusoh had been married for ten years and still had no offspring.

Young Dolah brought out the rice. Two plates of plain good quality rice, a saucer filled with grated coconut, five roasted fish, and a cup of thick black coffee each. Dogol wriggled about, trying to get comfortable. There was a brief silence.

'How was your meeting with Semaun?' Dogol asked, breaking the temporary quietness.

Pak Senik did not immediately reply. He bent over and rearranged the simple meal. He placed a plate of steamed rice in front of his guest, then sighed as he stirred the coffee. Dogol studied the village headman's face. When Pak Senik had settled down again, Dogol quickly repeated his question.

'Did Semaun agree to our scheme?'

'Pak Kasa died,' said Pak Senik.

The room became very still. Then a thin smile broke

across Dogol's lips. The smile was allowed to gradually broaden. Dogol had been waiting a long time to hear that.

'Did Semaun agree to our scheme?' Dogol asked again, deliberately making no reference to Pak Kasa's death.

Pak Senik was silent. He shook his head. The family had behaved atrociously. He would never forget how Semaun had threatened him. Despite his age, Pak Kasa had been very curt. But there was no point in telling that to someone like Dogol. His type only knew how to bark and snarl. They couldn't think past getting rid of Semaun and his family. They didn't have the intelligence to see that the family could be cured by peaceful means. None of them could see that. But Pak Senik was optimistic now. Semaun and his family were under an enormous obligation to him. Pak Senik was a patient man. He wouldn't lose hope. There was a great, secret bond between himself and Semaun's family. Dogol may not have approved, but Pak Senik sincerely believed that one day he could lead the family away from their errors to the path of righteousness.

'Does that mean none of us can participate because of those bastards?' Dogol demanded.

Pak Senik sipped at his hot coffee, before slowly placing the cup on the woven mat.

'That's impossible,' Dogol continued. 'They're standing in the way of progress.'

Pak Senik was upset. Although outwardly he remained calm, he was inwardly furious with those villagers who continued to oppose Semaun and his family. Dogol was one. Jusoh was just as bad. Their ideas went no further than having Semaun arrested. If they couldn't have him put in jail, they wanted him thrown out of the village. They didn't want stubborn people like Semaun in their village.

'I'll try again,' Pak Senik suddenly said, as though he

had not already done all he could to persuade Semaun. He knew Semaun was indebted to him.

'Try what?'

'To persuade Semaun to plant twice a year.'

Dogol bowed his head and ground his teeth together. He was outraged by Pak Senik's chatter. Why wouldn't he take firm action against that damned Semaun? His head remained bowed a long time, as he waited for his anger to ebb. It would be ridiculous if the rest of the village couldn't participate in the scheme because of Semaun. Perhaps Pak Senik and Pak Kasa were in league. Dogol wanted to kick Pak Senik in the head. He wanted to shout at him that he was a coward. He wanted to run down the stairs, get all the villagers, go to Semaun's house and burn it down. Reduce the house to ash. Dogol struggled to control himself. There was nothing to be gained by behaving like a fierce buffalo in another man's house so early in the morning.

'Don't you ever get tired of trying to persuade people?' Dogol suddenly asked.

'I haven't yet,' Pak Senik replied.

'The road would have been finished a long time ago if he hadn't tried to attack the labourers.'

'I know that,' Pak Senik replied. 'But the tractor knocked down one of his coconut trees. No one warned him beforehand.'

'He's always destroying other people's irrigation channels,' Dogol further accused.

'How many times did he do that?'

'Three.'

'Other people damaged his channels first. They started it.'

'Semaun crippled my cow.'

'Whose cow?'

'My cow.'

'Why do you think he did that?'

'Out of malice.'

'No.'
'Why, then?'
'Because you were unjust. I asked you to divide the cows out evenly. You didn't give Semaun one. Why not?'
Pak Senik seldom spoke in such a forthright manner. He was usually very self-controlled. Dolah and Pak Senik's wife began to fidget, afraid that Pak Senik and Dogol might come to blows.
'Semaun's a troublemaker.'
'He is not.'
'Yes, he is.'
'He isn't.'
'He is.'
'You forced him to be a troublemaker. You're the troublemaker, not Semaun.'
Dogol was possessed by blind rage. His head spun. He stared through a dark haze at a small axe resting in a niche in one of the corner pillars of the room, and felt an overwhelming urge to leap up and grab the axe by the handle. He was damned if anyone would call him, a man with a wife and family, a troublemaker. But then he saw Pak Senik's wife and Dolah staring at him through the doorway. They were obviously amazed; they had never seen Pak Senik treat a guest so harshly before, especially Dogol, who was virtually his constant companion.
Pak Senik stayed exactly where he was; he didn't even move an inch. He realized that Dogol was staring at the axe, but he wasn't particularly worried. His machette was still near the door, and it was longer and sharper than the axe. In fact, he doubted that Dogol would do anything as foolish as attack him. But if he did rush him, Pak Senik resolved to do nothing. Pak Senik believed that truth was on his side. He had been patient and kind with Semaun and it had paid off. Granted Dogol, Jusoh, Lebai Debasa and the other villagers

would not approve of what he had done, truth was truth, and it would prevail. And Pak Senik would prevail, even if everyone hated him.

Dogol stood up quickly and tightened his sarong around his waist. Without saying another word, he leapt down to the ground. He hurried along the deliberately unfinished clay road.

The red clay embankments on either side of the road seemed so close that they almost crushed his ribs. The ugly, broken mounds of earth infuriated him; they were like enemy forces, ready to ambush him. Dogol walked very quickly. Earlier that morning he had gone to Pak Senik's house gaily swinging a branch at the dew on the tips of the grass; now he rubbed his hands together in sheer rage. Every so often he threw a punch, as though there was something in the air taunting him. His chest, belly and head were taut with confusion. Pak Senik had changed, Dogol thought; he was no longer the calm, gentle person he used to be. Dogol was shocked. Pak Senik had threatened him; he knew about the way he had divided out the government cows. It was just as well that no one else had been present. It was just as well Jusoh and Lebai Debasa weren't there. Had they been, Dogol wouldn't have been able to hold his head up. His chest, belly and head tightened again; the conflict was very intense. Dogol quickened his pace, as though some mad dog was snapping at his legs. Perhaps Semaun, that wounded bull, had said something. Or he might have frightened Pak Senik, by threatening to plunge a knife in his shoulder. Dogol wondered if Pak Senik had talked to Semaun about the way that the cows were supposed to have been divided out. He put his hands to his head, afraid Semaun might attack him in the next few days. What if Pak Senik had discussed the matter with the other villagers? What would they do to him? What if he had gone and told Jusoh and Lebai Debasa? No! Pak Senik mustn't be allowed to go around telling everyone of the sorry mess Dogol had made of things. Dogol stopped and briefly studied the red clay road in front of him. His vision blurred. His head spun. Pak Senik mustn't reveal his secret. It was time the headman started getting tough with that damned Semaun. There had to be a way of getting him shoved into jail. And if there wasn't, then he would have to be forced out of the village. It didn't matter where he went. As long as he didn't hang around Banggul Derdap. Dogol sensed that Semaun could be a major obstacle to his ambitions; his own, deeply held, long cherished ambitions. Dogol started off again. His mind suddenly moved in another direction: to the healthy cows he had tethered in the long grass at the edge of the swamp. He decided to take them home as quickly as he could, and then to go to Lebai Debasa's house. He had to tell Lebai Debasa that Pak Senik had changed; he was on Semaun's side now. It was not a trivial matter. It was very, very important. It had serious implications for the future of the whole village. There was no time to waste. Pak Senik's weak, indecisive manner could only serve to incite Semaun to further deeds of violence; especially as Pak Senik was actually supporting him. Semaun's reign of terror was steadily moving towards its climax. If they didn't stop him, he would act like a fiend. He might hamstring their animals with the same ease that another man would cut a dye-shrub. He might break their irrigation channels at will. His behaviour would probably become even more outrageous. What if he started pestering the girls of the village? Or the men's wives and families? Semaun might look human, but in his heart he was no better than a savage dog. Dogol would be frank with Lebai Debasa. Pak Senik's weak, indecisive manner had made Semaun the vicious animal he was. If they wanted to stop Semaun, then they would first have to strike at the source of his viciousness. It was time Pak Senik was taught a lesson. And if he didn't want to learn, Dogol had no doubt that Lebai Debasa would agree to calling a meeting so that Pak Senik could be stripped of his position as village headman. The only way the village could live in peace would be to get rid of that wounded bull buffalo, Semaun. There would be no turning back once Jusoh and Lebai Debasa realized how misguided Pak Senik had been. After Pak Senik had been silenced, it would be easy enough to banish Semaun. As he pounded along the road, Dogol convinced himself that this was the only solution. Semaun was a wounded bull; he could go to hell. Pak Senik had made him what he was; he could go to hell as well. Dogol suddenly wondered who would replace Pak Senik as village headman. There was no obvious answer. But the answer was hidden deep inside him, in the furtherest recesses of his heart. Dogol smiled at the secret answer. Turning right, he started down the overgrown track. He strode through the long grass, with its rich store of various sized thorny bushes, like a holiday-maker paddling in the water at the seaside. He could feel the wounds forming as the thorns ripped into his flesh but he didn't care. A few leeches reached out for his legs; he ignored them. He kept on going. It was only a short distance to the clearing where he had tethered his cows. He would rip the stakes out and take the beasts home the quickest way he could. It was crucial he get to Lebai Debasa's house as soon as possible. He must waste no time in spreading the news that the two men were in league with each other. Pak Senik was encouraging Semaun's wild behaviour. The villagers were rich in nothing but their poverty; their interests were being betrayed.

When he reached the clearing, Dogol stopped suddenly. He stood there rigid, as though his feet had been nailed to the ground. The rapid beat of his heart became even more rapid. His chest rose and fell visibly. He looked frantically around him. One of the pregnant cows had gone. The other cow was gone too. His darling calves were no longer there. For a time Dogol stood where he was, completely unable to move. Then, suddenly, his eyes noticed large drops of blood on the flattened grass. He looked carefully at the lumps. Then he saw one of the stakes was missing. The other was still in the ground, with its rope attached, but the rope had been broken. Dogol moved suspiciously forward. On reaching the second stake, he bent over, pulled it out with a quick jerk, and then stood up again. He walked around trying to find the other stake. It wasn't there. Dogol stopped again. He wondered if he should look for his cows in the bushes on the edge of the thick jungle. Perhaps something had startled the animals. It seemed unlikely the rope would have broken so easily any other way. The animals must be in the undergrowth. They were probably lost and couldn't find their way out.

'What happened! What happened!' Dogol shouted, like a madman.

He let the complaint die away. For a few moments he was silent, as he tried to control himself. Perhaps some wild beast had come along the track and scared his cows. Perhaps a tiger had come out of the jungle at dawn; a hungry tiger. A hungry tiger could do anything. It could break the neck of a pregnant cow with the greatest ease. It could attack an animal far larger than itself. It could drag its victim far into the jungle, then wait until nightfall to tear it apart. Dogol began to feel uneasy. If a tiger had attacked his beasts, their corpses would now be deep inside the jungle. Dogol shifted his attention to the flattened grass. There had been a fierce struggle. He could imagine what the fight had been like. The pregnant cow, still tethered, and with the calf in its belly, doing everything it could' to defend itself against its enemy. The tiger would have had no difficulty leaping on the cow's back and hammering away at its gullet. The other cow standing by, watching, and, when it could take no more, running into the undergrowth with its rope flying in the air behind it. If his suspicions were correct, then the cow and the two calves were still somewhere in the bushes. Dogol's first instinct was to go to the village headman and tell him what had happened, so the villagers could find the tiger and kill it. But when he thought of how much Pak Senik had changed, he spat on the ground in disgust. Pak Senik was standing in his way; he was damned if he was going to ask him for help.

'Perhaps some person deliberately startled the animals and killed one of them,' Dogol suddenly thought. The unexpected possibility made his heart pound even more rapidly than before. He imagined Semaun's resentful features. Semaun had held a grudge against him ever since he had missed out on getting one of the government cows. Of course some human beings had viciously mistreated the poor, innocent creatures. Semaun had probably spent the previous day unsuccessfully waiting for an opportunity to attack the beasts, then followed him to the swamp earlier that morning, Dogol decided. He had waited in the bushes until Dogol was at Pak Senik's house, then come out of hiding with his knife in his hand, and plunged its silver blade into the pregnant cow's neck. The animal had collapsed to the ground, gasping for air. The confused scenes flicked quickly through Dogol's mind. Semaun must have done it, with Pak Senik's backing. This further strengthened his resolve to get rid of Pak Senik; the old man no longer deserved to be village headman. Without thinking any further about the matter, Dogol waded into the undergrowth and rushed noisily along under the trees. Startled birds flew into the air, looking for other shelter. Dogol continued pushing his way through the bushes, eager to get to Lebai Debasa's house as quickly as possible. Here was another example of Pak Senik encouraging Semaun's viciousness which everyone in the village ought to know. He was even more determined now. The proof was mounting. Pak Senik had been rude to him and had gone over to Semaun's side. Not only that, his cows had been hamstrung. Worse, one of his cows had actually been killed, while it was still carrying a calf. These acts of violence clearly showed how cruel and inhumane Semaun was. He was becoming increasingly brutal as well. Dogol had to warn Lebai Debasa, Jusoh and all the other villagers. It was essential that something be done at once. Pak Senik had to be punished. They had to hunt Semaun down. If they couldn't catch him, then they would set fire to his shack. The villagers wouldn't have to think twice when he showed them the evidence. Burn damned Semaun's shack to a charred frame. Burn the shack to the ground. Burn the walls, roof, and support posts to ash.

Dogol forced his way through the undergrowth. He was approaching the high ground. Despite his shortness of breath, he plunged onwards through the bushes.

On reaching Lebai Debasa's house, he screamed as loudly as he could. Because he was panting heavily, his voice sounded like water rushing across a series of rocks.

'Lebai Debasa!' he roared.

Lebai Debasa appeared from within the house. When he realized that the breathless creature was his dear old friend, he raised his eyebrows a little, then grabbed his white skullcap from its usual position on a nail in a support beam, and came quickly outside onto the bamboo platform. The poles rattled noisily as he walked across them, rather like a truck passing over a small bridge. He climbed down the stairs. Dogol was exhausted.

'What's wrong?' he asked, massaging his friend's chest with his right hand.

Despite the brevity of the question, Dogol could not give an immediate answer. He was breathing too heavily to be able to speak properly. Lebai Debasa realized this and massaged his heaving chest again.

'What's wrong?' he repeated.

Dogol slowly turned around and put his right hand on Lebai Debasa's shoulder, as though trying to support himself.

'It's Semaun,' replied Dogol.

The moment he heard the name of that wild bull, Lebai Debasa stopped massaging Dogol. He put his hand behind his back. On discovering that his sheath was not there, he sprinted up the stairs and snatched his machette from its hook. He tied the machette around his waist, knotting the rope precisely in front of his navel. The machette had a handle of *sintok* root; Lebai Debasa touched it to give himself courage. When he was satisfied that everything was in place, he went over to Dogol again. Dogol had caught his breath a little by then.

'What's wrong?' he asked, as though he had completely forgotten Dogol's answer.

'It's Semaun,' Dogol repeated for the second time.

Lebai Debasa frowned.

'Semaun killed my cow.'

Lebai Debasa's jaw dropped. Dogol could see small pieces of betel nut and reddened lime in the cracks between his teeth.

'The cow was pregnant,' Dogol added, stressing the word 'pregnant' slightly.

'He's a swine,' Lebai Debasa suddenly snarled. 'Is he still there?'

'Who?'

'Who do you think?'

'Semaun?'

Lebai Debasa nodded.

'He's gone. So has the cow. This is all that was left.' Dogol whipped the rope and peg off his left shoulder.

'How do you know it was that bastard?'

'I don't,' Dogol said. 'But there's no one else in Banggul Derdap who would dare cut a cow's throat. First he attacked their legs. Now he does whatever he likes. He cut the cow's throat.'

'What about the carcase?' Lebai Debasa suddenly asked him.

'It's gone. He must have dragged it into the forest, skinned it, and taken the meat away. He's probably sold the lot by now.'

'Sold ritually impure meat?'

'How would anyone know it was impure?' replied Dogol. 'No one in town would know that. They don't care anyway, as long as it's meat. Semaun's type isn't even afraid of God any more.'

There was a brief silence. Lebai Debasa patted his forehead with his hand.

'Have you told Pak Senik?'

The very name of the man who had just abused him made Dogol jump. But he made sure Lebai Debasa couldn't see his reaction, because he didn't want to give him the wrong impression. He would have to be guarded about his new attitude towards Pak Senik, if he wanted to win the Lebai's confidence. People would believe anything he said about Semaun, but it would be much harder convincing them that Pak Senik had changed. Dogol spent a few minutes thinking about what he ought to say next.

'Have you told the headman?' Lebai Debasa repeated, when he found Dogol struck dumb.

'No!' replied Dogol, in a very cursory manner.

'Wasn't he home?'

Dogol remained silent.

'Do you know where he's gone?'

'He was home,' Dogol replied. 'I've just come from there. He threw me out.'

The statement shocked Lebai Debasa. He stared at Dogol in disbelief. The old man would never treat a guest like that. He had always been scrupulously polite at home. Lebai Debasa's reaction forced Dogol to continue immediately.

'He's backing Semaun now. Pak Senik doesn't want

to plant twice a year either. Perhaps he's scared of standing up to Semaun. When Pak Kasa died, Pak Senik prayed for him and took part in the funeral procession.'

Lebai Debasa thought for a while. The whole business worried him. How could Pak Senik have changed so quickly? The old man was very dependent on Dogol; why should he chase him out of his house, like a mangy cat? Lebai Debasa was torn between belief and disbelief. Pak Senik couldn't possibly abandon the new planting scheme so easily. It was a major project. Everyone in the village would benefit. It would lead to happiness and prosperity. Pak Senik wouldn't abandon the project just because of Semaun. Something else must have set the old man off. Perhaps they'd talked about the division of the cows. At that, Lebai Debasa looked up, as if to show that he had understood the situation. Dogol quickly started talking again.

'Of course you know,' he said, 'Pak Senik has never really supported us. I wanted Semaun arrested. You wanted him thrown out of the village. Jusoh agreed. The whole village would have been glad to see the wounded bull gone. Pak Senik was too weak. He wouldn't do a thing.'

Dogol finished his speech, then glanced cautiously at Lebai Debasa, who was standing beside him. He studied the Lebai's face. He was keen that Lebai Debasa should share his hatred for Pak Senik. Dogol watched him for a long time. Suddenly his lips broke into a faint smile; Lebai Debasa had slowly started nodding his head. Dogol's arguments were gradually starting to have an effect.

'Do you know why he didn't want to get rid of Semaun?' asked Dogol.

Lebai Debasa blinked.

'Do you know why he didn't want to have Semaun arrested?'

Lebai Debasa's mouth still hung open.

'Do you know why people are always fighting with each other in Banggul Derdap?'

Lebai Debasa continued to gape.

Dogol gave him no time to think. Lebai Debasa's silence was clear proof that Dogol's darts had gone deep into his heart. Dogol quickly resumed his attack.

'Because Pak Senik is a coward. Because he hasn't got enough confidence in himself to give the district the leadership it deserves. That is why he's always putting things off. That's why he won't crush that stinging-nettle, Semaun.'

As he spoke, Dogol was reminded of his cows. His heart missed a beat. He wondered if Lebai Debasa knew about the way he had divided out the government cows. But then he drove the thought out of his head by demanding, 'We must do something before the village itself is crippled.'

'Perhaps Pak Senik did have a hand in what happened to your cows,' Lebai Debasa butted in.

'The dead pregnant cow?'

'Hmm. Perhaps Pak Senik is in league with Semaun.'

Dogol did not agree with him straight away, although he was considerably relieved. Very slowly Dogol nodded his head.

'We must call Jusoh right away,' continued Lebai Debasa.

Dogol remained silent; he was sure Lebai Debasa could deal with Semaun and Pak Senik.

'We must tell the Imam as well.'

Dogol still said nothing.

'We must tell Jusoh, the Imam, and everyone in the whole village,' Lebai Debasa continued, as he started to walk away. He strode towards the rear of his house. Dogol watched him for a while, then started following him. But before he could move ten paces, he stopped. Lebai Debasa had started shouting the names of the various villagers.

'Jusoh! Jusoh! Jusoh!'
'Hamad! Hamad! Hamad!'
'Berahim! Deris! Haya! Usin!'

Lebai Debasa's booming voice bounced against the hills. His voice crackled with the same harshness the guardians of the field use when they chase marauding wild pigs away from the new grain. Lebai Debasa kept on shouting the men's names until the air around Banggul Derdap was entirely filled with the sound of his voice.

Dogol stood calmly behind him. He knew Lebai Debasa's patience had snapped. Semaun didn't deserve to live in Banggul Derdap. He had to be either crushed or driven out. He could go and live in another village. Which village, didn't matter. As long as they got rid of him, right away; that was all that mattered. It was none of their business where he went. What about Pak Senik? There was no way they could destroy him. Nor could he be driven out of the village. The most Dogol could hope would be to weaken the villagers' faith in the old man. Once their trust cracked, Dogol could gradually widen the breach until the villagers no longer believed in him at all. Pak Senik's tolerance had gone too far. It wasn't right to keep on making concessions to someone like Semaun. Pak Senik and his kind were only holding back the government's development programme. It was time the villagers stopped believing in Pak Senik. It was time they knew the real truth.

'Jusoh! Jusoh! Jusoh!'

Lebai Debasa's voice boomed out again. Without waiting for the echoes to die away, he continued shouting the other men's names.

'Hamad! Hamad! Hamad!'

His voice roared out, reverberating against the hills which surrounded the village. And, again, he did not let the echoes die away, but added to them by continuing to shout:

'Berahim! Deris! Haya! Usin!'

His voice seemed to be tearing away at his throat. Suddenly his cry was taken up by other voices all over Banggul Derdap. Then, from all over the village, people came running. The volley of shouts surely meant someone wanted help. Someone was in trouble. Perhaps Lebai Debasa's family had been entered by nature spirits. Perhaps all the rice in their barn had been stolen. Perhaps Semaun had run amok again, now that his father was dead. Folks came scampering from the sunrise side of the village, leaping along the rice-field walls like monkeys with red ants on their tails. The scene was repeated on the sunset side of the village. The situation was suddenly very confused. Lebai Debasa kept shouting for Jusoh, Imam Hamad, and the other men. The villagers kept shouting back, then matching their calls with action. They left their houses, taking with them whatever weapons they could find. Something was seriously wrong at Lebai Debasa's house. They had no alternative but to do everything they could to help. When one suffered, all suffered. If one was happy, all of them were happy.

Jusoh grabbed a hoe handle which was leaning against his stairs. He swung the six foot length of wood in the air as he ran along. The Imam bounded towards the house, without his turban. The rolls of fat around his belly shook as he leapt over the irrigation gates along the rice-field walls. A hunk of wood as thick as a five-year-old child's arm was loosely clutched in his right hand. Those villagers who were still working in their fields, scattered, wading quickly through the water, and started running helter-skelter. They all had one goal: Lebai Debasa's house. There could be no ignoring his call.

Dogol stayed exactly where he was, carefully watching the haste and confusion. A number of direct and simple schemes suggested themselves to him. He was comforted by the thought of how easily the villagers could be swayed. When everyone arrived, he was sure Lebai Debasa would explain the whole thing to them. He was totally reliant on Lebai Debasa; if everything worked out as he hoped it would, he would make Lebai Debasa his right-hand man. The Lebai was the most talented person in the district.

Dogol would merely have to tell them which path to take. Once Lebai Debasa had finished, Dogol would lead the mob. They would rush to Semaun's house, then throw a fire-brand at it. Dogol would make sure that one of the quick-tempered villagers took a brand. The fire would make short work of the woven bamboo walls and the split-palm roof. Everyone in the house would be burnt to death at once. Or, if he or she tried to stop the mob, so much the worse for them. Dogol didn't care. This was bigger than any one person. The whole of Banggul Derdap was involved. No particular individual could be blamed. The majority opinion was what mattered in today's society. If the villagers didn't like Semaun, then Semaun would have to go. They would kill him if he tried to stand in their way. They would burn his house down. His mother and pretty sister would suffer the same fate. Of course Pak Senik would rush to Semaun's house as soon as he saw the angry mob making its way there. He would scream at them when he saw the torch. But it would make no difference. Once aroused, the masses could not be stopped. There would be no point in pleading with them. If Pak Senik tried to hold them back, they would punish him too for defying the will of the people.

Dogol toyed excitedly with the ideas in his head. He knew exactly what he must do when everyone arrived.

'Semaun killed Dogol's pregnant cow,' Lebai Debasa explained to each person who had come running in response to his call. The news spread quickly. There was no need to say who Semaun was. Everybody knew.

Each person he told sighed, then shook his or her head. The Imam stood rooted to the spot, puffing heavily. He was overwhelmed with anger at the viciously cruel things Semaun had done to the poor, innocent beast. His jaw dropped for several minutes.

'Semaun's been allowed to run wild for too long. It's time the wretch was stopped!' Lebai Debasa thrust his clenched fist into the air. 'He has tyrannized us long enough!'

The villagers looked at each other. Craning their necks, a few of them peered around as though they had lost something.

'What about Pak Senik?' asked a voice from among the tightly packed crowd.

Dogol nervously scanned the villagers, trying to decide who had asked the question. He had no wish to consult Pak Senik. However, his nervousness quickly ebbed as he listened to Lebai Debasa's answer.

'Pak Senik is too weak; he won't stand up to Semaun and he doesn't want us to either. This isn't the first time Semaun has run wild, but he's never killed any animals before. The next thing we know, he'll be molesting our wives and children. We just can't give in to him the way Pak Senik does! It's time we did something ourselves!'

By the end of the speech, the last traces of Dogol's nervousness had completely vanished. The villagers seemed fully convinced by the answer. Pak Senik behaves like a woman, Dogol thought to himself. He never disagrees with anyone. Not that he ought to be aggressive all the time, but there should be some limits to the extent one person could accommodate himself to what everyone else wanted. If Semaun insisted on walking all over us, then there was no point in attempting further compromise with him. Something had to be done. If no single person felt confident enough to fight him, they'd send two people. If two people wouldn't do it, they'd send three. Or, as things stood, the whole village could go. No one was invincible. Semaun certainly wasn't. He was human; he could be beaten. And, sooner or later, he would be.

'Pak Senik can't be trusted,' Dogol said as he moved to Lebai Debasa's side. 'He's a coward!'

The sudden statement drew everyone's eyes to Dogol. Pak Senik was a very influential man. Dogol had to be careful how he played his cards. He would have to choose his words well if he wanted to achieve his hidden ambition.

'We hate Semaun,' Dogol continued. 'He's a violent person, and he has disturbed the peacefulness of our village many times. Each time, Pak Senik has asked us to be patient—we were patient. Semaun went on the rampage again. Pak Senik asked us to be patient yet again. Once again we were patient. Now he's slashed the cow's throat, killing not only the cow but also the calf in its belly. A poor, little calf, which hasn't even tasted the green grass. How long are we going to let Pak Senik boss us about? How long must we be patient? How long will it be before Semaun starts molesting our wives and children?'

Dogol spoke with such sincerity that beads of sweat formed on his forehead. He unrolled the top of his sarong and wiped his brow.

There was a brief silence, in which the only sound was the villagers' heavy breathing. Dogol studied the sweating faces in front of him. Suddenly the voice he had been waiting for emerged from the crowd of wet faces.

'Semaun's a swine! Let's burn his house down!'

Dogol looked up, wondering who had shouted. But before he could do anything, the cry was on the lips of the other villagers.

'Let's burn his house down!'
'Let's burn his house down!'
'Let's burn his house down!'

The cry was repeated three times. The sound was like thunder. Even more terrifying, the villagers waved their weapons each time they called out. Hoe handles, pieces of wood, weed-cutters, *samak* roots, sharpened bamboo poles, all waved together in the air. The first time they screamed, Dogol simply smiled. His darts had obviously struck home. The second and third times the villagers screamed, he joined in. He opened his mouth wide and shook his fist.

After the shouting stopped, there was still a considerable uproar. The villagers talked among themselves. Dogol patted Lebai Debasa on the back. Lebai Debasa turned around. When he saw Dogol's face, he nodded.

'Everybody follow us!' Lebai Debasa called.

The cry was greeted with a loud cheer. Dogol walked in front of the crowd. He gradually quickened his pace as he realized that the villagers were jostling each other behind him, impatient to proceed more rapidly. They charged along the narrow track, knocking down the overhanging clumps of grass on both sides of the path. *Keman* thorns caught in the hairs of their legs. Sharp prickles covered the ground. Dozens of hard, cracked, calloused heels smashed the coarse grass on the track to a pulp. They ignored all this. They kept on going. And Dogol led them. It's not very far to Semaun's house now, Dogol thought to himself as the confusion swirled around him. We'll be there before long. No matter what, nothing could stop Semaun's house from being reduced to a smouldering heap of ashes. What could Semaun do when he saw the dozens of villagers attacking his house? Nothing. He would be too frightened. His courage and ferocity would turn sour on him. Oh, the brave, strong man would show what a coward he was when he saw the waves of humanity rushing his home. Dogol was keen to watch the wounded bull's expression change when that happened. The villagers, too, would want to see his face then. Semaun was supposed to be invincible; it would be a pleasure to watch him turn pale as the angry mob surged forward. There would be dozens of people there, an impressive number. Dogol imagined himself screaming for Semaun to come outside. He would get Semek and Semaun's mother out on the bamboo platform as well. The whole village could look at them. It would be the last time they would see them. Next Dogol would urge some of the more spirited members of the crowd to seize Semaun and his family, and bind them to the coconut trees near the house. Then he would give the order for the fire-brand to be thrown on the roof. The flames would attack the dry, thatched roof with the same eagerness a hungry man devours a plate of mushy rice. The angry flames would run wild, leaping high into the air. He imagined the black smoke, full of soot, swirling about like a cloud of lost flying-ants. How the villagers would laugh as they stood about in the yard! He would leave Semaun and his family tied to the trees so they could watch the fire. The fire would be as merciless as Semaun himself. Dogol's thoughts were suddenly interrupted by the sight of Semaun's front gate. Dogol summoned up his courage. His followers' cheers grew louder and louder. They knew they had almost reached Semaun's house. They were about a hundred paces away from the gate.

We'll flatten the gate, Dogol thought, and trample down the young banana trees along the path. If anyone wants the trunks later, he can feed them to his water-buffaloes. The villagers would rush right in.

They rushed through the gate, breaking the posts. Both Dogol and Lebai Debasa led the raiding party. Suddenly Dogol gave the order to stop. Lebai Debasa raised his hand into the air. Jusoh ran forward, waving his hoe handle, and stood beside Dogol. There was neither hide nor hair of Tok Imam to be seen; perhaps he was lost somewhere among the sturdy bunch of youths. The loud shout which had accompanied them all the way, suddenly faded. The atmosphere became very oppressive. They were breathing heavily; their hearts pounded loudly within them. Each person stared at the tiny house, with its thatched roof and woven walls. They stood where they were, stunned. It was not the house which had affected them. On the rough bamboo platform outside the house stood Semaun, with a long, single-bladed knife across his right shoulder. The silver blade glinted each time it caught the sunlight. Semaun waited for the mob to arrive. His house was as precious as his father, Semaun thought; to burn one was to burn the other. He would die, rather than have his home turned to swirling ashes.

But it was not Semaun who had thrown the marauding villagers into such a panic. They were not afraid of Semaun, the wounded bull buffalo. It made no difference to them whether he carried a chopper, a wood-cutter, a grass-cutter, a machette, or a magic sword. Another man stood on Semaun's left: Pak Senik, headman of the turbulent Banggul Derdap.

Semaun stood motionless; Pak Senik was far less steady. He held his headband in his hands, and nothing else. He was obviously not equipped for a fight. Nevertheless, he waited for them to arrive.

Dogol's face turned a ghastly shade of white as soon as he saw Pak Senik. He was afraid of the influence Pak Senik could have over the villagers. The old man might win them over to his side, leaving Dogol alone in the middle of the yard. He was terrified Pak Senik might want to discuss how he had shared out the government cows. All his carefully constructed schemes would come tumbling down if the villagers listened to Pak Senik.

He turned to look at Lebai Debasa. Lebai Debasa stared back at him. Dogol shifted his gaze to Jusoh. Jusoh stared back at him as well. Dogol was thrown into even greater chaos. He was so reliant on them that he

was unable to meet the fierce gleam in their eyes.
His long suppressed deceit and dishonesty struggled to express itself. He knew he had done wrong. Semaun hadn't killed his cow. His face went pale again. He started to breathe more heavily. All the villagers loved Pak Senik; he knew he could never turn them against the old man.
Dogol turned towards the crowd. He was deeply moved by their eyes. Fear and guilt overwhelmed him again. He thought of his own deception in dividing the government cows. He thought of how he had lied so that the villagers would want to get rid of Semaun. Dogol became even more afraid. But only he knew how dishonest he had been. No one else knew. Neither Lebai Debasa, nor Jusoh; not even Tok Imam. None of the villagers knew the tactics he had employed.
'We want Semaun!' he screamed when he could stand it no longer. They mustn't discover how dishonest he had been. He would fight them on the basis of his dishonesty. All the great heroes had won because they were more cunning than their enemies.
'We want Semaun!' he repeated loudly. All eyes focused on the two men on the bamboo platform.
Semaun turned towards Pak Senik. The old man shook his head.
'Don't go, Semaun,' his mother called from where she stood, pressed against the wall.
'Do what Pak Senik says,' she advised.
Semaun did not speak. He did not even gesture.
Suddenly the villagers started screaming Semaun's name and waving their weapons. A few of them could be heard swearing obscenely.
'Why?' Pak Senik shouted, lifting his headcloth. His shout was swallowed up in the din.
'Why?' he repeated, more loudly. The scene gradually became quiet.
'Why do you want Semaun?' he added.

'Because he's a troublemaker!' someone shouted from among the crowd.

'Burn his house down!' someone else called out.

'Burn! Burn! Burn!' they chanted. Burn the house and burn Semaun, body and soul. Semaun would never let them ravage what the ancestors had given him. He didn't care how small the house was. Had it been ten storeys tall, he couldn't have loved it more. He had built the house with his own hands. He had planed the support posts for five days and nights. He had spent three afternoons in the jungle collecting the thatch. Semaun, his father, his mother and his sister, had plaited the walls together. It was his house; built with the sweat of his brow. Mak Leha was positive he wouldn't let a crazed mob destroy the house. He would jump down and lay into them with his long-bladed knife before that happened. Violence never settled anything, as far as she was concerned.

'What has he done wrong?' Pak Senik shouted again.

'He killed Dogol's cow,' replied Lebai Debasa.

'The cow was pregnant,' Jusoh continued.

'Burn! Burn! Burn!' the crowd called out.

Semaun was shocked. He looked at Pak Senik, then shook his head. Semek and Mak Leha were stunned.

'Whose cow was it?' Pak Senik asked.

'My cow,' replied Dogol.

'Where did this happen?'

'At the edge of the swamp.'

'Is the carcase still there?'

Dogol did not reply. He wasn't sure. Certainly he hadn't looked very hard for it. But a man who lives by deceit is never short of an answer.

'It's gone,' he replied.

'Gone where?'

'You'll have to ask Semaun.'

Pak Senik turned to Semaun. The youth shook his head.

'Semaun skinned the beast,' a voice called out. 'He sold the meat.'

Semaun leapt down to the ground. His eyes shone as he searched for the person who had dared accuse him of such an impropriety. But Pak Senik wasn't prepared to see blood spilt. The villagers had been tricked. Pak Senik knew who was to blame. He had known all along. But he didn't want to use force. He wanted to work the matter out gradually, if possible. Leaping down to the ground, he took hold of Semaun's arm. Semaun offered no resistance; he allowed the old man to hold him back. Pak Senik whispered something in Semaun's ear. Semaun nodded.

'Let's go and look for the carcase,' Pak Senik shouted. 'It's the only way we can decide who's right and who's wrong. If we don't find the carcase, we'll burn Semaun's house down. We'll let it burn until only the charred uprights remain.'

There was a brief calm. Pak Senik studied the villagers' faces as they whispered to each other. Lebai Debasa turned to Dogol, but Dogol immediately turned away. He dared not meet anyone else's eyes. He could scarcely breathe. What if they find the carcase of the cow? Where could he run? The villagers would never trust him again. But he dared not argue with the village headman for fear of giving himself away.

'Burn! Burn! Burn!' Dogol screamed. His heart shrank within him when no one else took up the cry. The villagers were as silent as rocks. Slowly he turned to Lebai Debasa and nodded, hoping that, by the grace of God, the carcase really had gone.

'We'll do as Pak Senik suggests,' Lebai Debasa said, once he had secured Dogol's agreement. 'But Semaun must come with us.'

The sense of confusion returned to Banggul Derdap. The men started to run in different directions again. The children looked up in surprise. The women wondered what was happening. The sun shone white on the waters in the rice-fields. The raiding party ran across the retaining walls, led by Pak Senik. He was closely followed by Semaun, Dogol, Lebai Debasa and Jusoh. Pak Senik travelled as quickly as he could. He was not afraid. He knew Semaun was innocent. Pak Senik knew who was to blame, and it wasn't Semaun. The headman swore to himself that he would help that person to realize what he had done wrong.

They pounded across the walls. From time to time someone missed his footing and stepped in the muddy water. The water formed small ripples. From a distance, the ripples resembled scales on a fish.

When they reached the other side of the fields, they surged forward again. And despite his age, Pak Senik still led the way. He was very fast. His calves were covered with mud.

'Which way?' he asked.

'To the edge of the swamp,' replied Lebai Debasa.

'The edge of the swamp? No one ever tethers beasts there.'

Pak Senik felt more relaxed. No one ever went to the edge of the marsh. The forest was very thick there and the grass was lush. Pak Senik was sure Semaun hadn't killed the cow if it had really been tethered at the edge of the swamp. Something else must have happened to the beast. Pak Senik felt that it was important to hide his confidence. He wanted them to see what had happened with their own eyes. He wanted the whole village to see. Dogol had to see as well. Pak Senik wanted to watch Dogol's expression change when the time came.

They had now reached the new, unfinished road. The red clay stuck to the soles of their feet. The rich colour and the beautiful smell of the red clay mixed with the slushy mud were delightful. But nobody noticed. They kept on walking.

'What if we do find the carcase in the jungle?' Pak

Senik wondered. He thought of Dogol. Lying was taboo in Banggul Derdap. And this was no trivial affair; it could determine whether a man lived or died. What if the villagers turned on Dogol? What if they hacked him to pieces? Pak Senik was reluctant to consider the matter too closely.

His quiet self-confidence suddenly disappeared. They had reached the clearing. Some of the grass had been grazed and flattened. Large splashes of blood mingled with the green blades of grass.

'Everybody into the forest,' Pak Senik ordered. 'Spread out!'

They rushed into the forest, forcing their way along old abandoned tracks wherever possible, and through the undergrowth. It was crucial the carcase be found, so that they could decide who was innocent and who was not. There was a continual din. Some of the villagers screamed to each other about various things. Others shouted to drive any wild beasts away. The voices echoed against the harsh, tall hills.

Pak Senik made his own way into the scrub. Whenever the branches became too dense for him, he dropped to the ground and crawled along, looking for footprints. So far he had found nothing.

Suddenly he heard a loud shout. Stopping, he tried to determine from which direction the call had come. There was another shout:

'I've found it! I've found it! I've found it!'

The cry reverberated against the hills. Pak Senik immediately started shoving his way through the jungle; he wanted to get there first, before anyone lost control of himself and did something wrong.

By the time Pak Senik arrived, the villagers had already surrounded the carcase. He pushed his way through the human circle. What he saw shocked him.

The animal no longer looked like an animal at all. Her skin had been torn to shreds. The flesh of one thigh was missing. The belly was torn open, disgorging the animal's intestines and the calf, which was still smeared with amniotic fluid, in a confused heap on the ground. There were claw marks around the cow's neck. Pak Senik took hold of the animal by the horns and lifted; the neck was broken.

'Father Stripes,' the headman announced, ending the mystery.

'A tiger?' one of the villagers asked in surprise.

Most of the crowd nodded.

Suddenly a youth leapt out of the circle and jumped on top of the carcase, swinging a long-bladed chopper. It was Semaun.

'Where's Dogol? He said I killed his cow. He said I skinned her. He said I sold ritually impure meat.'

The farmers looked right and left, trying to find the liar known as Dogol. The fickle villagers had completely changed their attitude.

'Kill him!' someone screamed, waving a large machette.

The cry was taken up by every person there.

'Kill him! Kill him! Kill him!'

Pak Senik uneasily looked around for the man named Dogol but he was nowhere to be seen.

Lebai Debasa hurried into the middle of the circle. His mouth hung open but he was unable to speak.

'Kill him! Kill him! Kill him!'

The cry grew louder. Lebai Debasa, too, was waving his hands in the air. Jusoh moved to the centre of the circle and whispered something to Pak Senik's ear. The village headman nodded.

'Dogol's run away,' Pak Senik said. Lebai Debasa and Jusoh looked up in amazement, not really understanding what was happening.

'He's gone,' someone else said.

'After him!'

'We'll cut him to pieces!'

'Kill him!'

'Kill! Kill! Kill!'

The wind went out of Pak Senik. He was stunned. Once the fire of the villagers' wrath had been kindled, it would be no easy matter to extinguish the flames. Terror gripped him. He was frightened the farmers might scatter and run to Dogol's house. Frightened they might burn Dogol's house to the ground. He didn't want anything that horrible happening in his village. Pak Senik thought back to the Second World War. A couple of Japanese soldiers had lost their way. The villagers cut their throats. The villagers knew no fear, especially when they thought they were safe from the prying eyes of a government which was itself cruel and arbitrary.

When he realized how devious Dogol had been, Pak Senik felt angry too. He was tempted to send the villagers to Dogol's house himself. He thought of how cunningly Dogol had shared the cows out. Of how cunningly he had convinced the villagers that Semaun was a rowdy and a bully. Of how maliciously Dogol had tried to destroy his own standing as village headman. As he struggled to control himself, he was forced, once again, to reiterate his old standpoint.

'We must try to be patient. Dogol has done wrong. He'll be punished. God will punish him.'

Pak Senik looked around as he ended his brief speech. First he looked at Semaun, who still had one foot on the head of the dead cow. Semaun bowed his head. He shifted his gaze to Lebai Debasa and Jusoh; they looked away, as though afraid his eyes might contain some terrible curse. The villagers started to glance at each other; no one spoke.

They understood his patient manner. It had not always been to their taste, but they had gradually come to realize that his restraint was not a sign of weakness. He was not a coward. He could be angry when it was necessary. And when he was, no one could stop him.

'It's time to go,' Pak Senik said, once he was sure

everyone had accepted his advice. 'Go home, all of you. Leave Dogol to me. I'll find him and see what he has to say for himself. He'll be fully punished for what he has done.'

The villagers began to leave, walking slowly at first, and then increasingly quickly once they were on the track away from the swamp. Semaun looked at Pak Senik. The old man came over to him and patted him on the shoulder. The youth smiled and left with everyone else.

Pak Senik was upset by the quarrel. He had always wanted the villagers to live in harmony with each other. What had happened today would leave deep scars in Banggul Derdap. He was disgusted by Dogol's behaviour, over the cows and towards Semaun. Dogol could no longer be trusted. What an arrogant man he was; his nose almost touched the sky. Pak Senik thought of Lebai Debasa, Dogol's constant companion. Dogol was vile. He had schemed to catch Lebai Debasa in his trap, and had been most successful. Why had they never tried to resolve their disagreement with Semaun? And what about Jusoh; where did he stand in all this? These three men were the backbone of the village; what did the future hold? He was getting old. Although his voice was still strong, it was not as strong as it had been when he was younger. He shivered. Perhaps Lebai Debasa and Jusoh still had some scheme in mind, despite their smiles. What if they intended to weaken his position in Banggul Derdap? All men's hearts beat the same, yet all contain different motives. He was troubled by what might happen to a lonely, old man. His dreams for the progress of the village would disappear, like ground coconut pulp scattered in the wind; anything remaining would be gradually eaten by the hens. What if Dogol became village headman? What would happen to Semaun and his family then? And what about biannual planting? Pak Senik sighed, despairing of what could happen to Banggul Derdap when he no longer held the reins. Anxiously he started to walk home. No matter what happened, he was determined to remain true to his beliefs.

5
The Tiger

Pak Senik was still surprised at how quickly the mood of the village had changed. The villagers' attitude to Dogol was now completely different. Before long, someone would surely be insisting that Dogol ought to be driven out of Banggul Derdap. Pak Senik thought of Lebai Debasa. He thought of Jusoh. That was the sort of thing they might say. The Imam would agree with them as a matter of course. It was amazing the ease with which the two men had changed their mind. Not that they were ever very consistent. Despite that, Pak Senik was not prepared to interfere; he wanted to see how far the men would go.

Regardless of what anyone said or did, Dogol must not be expelled from Banggul Derdap. He had lived here a long time. It was his home. Pak Senik was conscious of the need to make Dogol fully aware of what he had done. He was also aware of his responsibility for Semaun. It was time Semaun and the villagers were on better terms again. Pak Senik would be even more delighted if Dogol and Semaun could be brought together again. If those two giants could be reunited, the stability of the village was guaranteed. Stability would mean happiness and the opportunity to implement a whole range of schemes. Pak Senik didn't want the biannual planting project abandoned just because of a misunderstanding between Semaun and Dogol. The headman was confident now that Semaun would do as he asked. He hoped Dogol would also obey him. Peace was his only desire. When the village was at peace, his duty would be done. And with his duty done, Pak Senik would be ready to face death calmly and confidently.

Dogol's problem was by no means solved. It was linked with the tiger and its attack on the cow. Pak Senik was sure that the tiger would return to finish the carcase, and that once it had tasted succulent cow's flesh, it would want more. Four or five days would suffice for the first carcase. Then the tiger would take another. And that too would eventually be gone. Pak Senik knew what a savage tiger could do. It would prowl about, roaring angrily, until its hunger was satisfied. It would attack humans. The villagers would be severely restricted in their movements; they wouldn't be able to go into the jungle to collect cane. The tiger had to be killed.

There was something that Pak Senik didn't know. Another person also wanted to finish the tiger. Dogol. It was something he had decided as soon as he rushed home. He must kill the tiger. He must take the corpse to Pak Senik's house. If he didn't show how brave he was, as soon as possible, all the villagers would despise him for the rest of his life.

That night, torches appeared here and there again in the village. Pak Senik had spent the day inviting the senior members of Banggul Derdap to his house, to discuss ways of destroying the ferocious tiger. Lebai Debasa and Jusoh were the first to arrive. Their torches had burnt brightly as they crossed the fields. But Pak Senik was not yet ready to begin the meeting. There was still one more person to come: Semaun. He had no doubt Semaun would come.

Senick lit Semaun's torch for him. Once the end of the torch was blazing strongly, she gave it to her brother.

He took it from her with a smile. After his first few steps, he suddenly stopped and felt for something near his waist. There was nothing there. He had forgotten his long knife.

'Semek!' he called out.

Semek appeared at the door, with her mother behind her.

'What is it?' his mother asked.

'My knife. I forgot my knife.'

Without waiting for any further instructions, Semek ran into the house and returned with the long-bladed chopper. Semaun took the weapon. His eyes sparkled in the light of the fire-brand.

'Where are you going?' his mother asked, although she already knew he had been invited to Pak Senik's house.

'To Pak Senik's.'

'Don't get lost on the way.'

Semaun knew what his mother was getting at. She was concerned that he might go somewhere else; Dogol's place, for instance. Semaun nodded and started for the path to the rice-fields. Two pairs of eyes hopefully watched him go. His mother and Semek, his sister. Semaun's torch shone fiercely as he strode, step by step, across the rice-fields. His knife swung rhythmically by his side. From time to time he lifted his hand away from the top of the weapon and threw a punch into the air to work off some of his youthful energy. The wind whistled past his hand.

He had no idea what Pak Senik wanted to talk about; he couldn't even guess what it might be. If Pak Senik wanted to discuss planting two crops a year, then Semaun felt he would have no alternative but to agree. It would mean breaking with ancestral custom. But he could scarcely refuse Pak Senik, considering what the old man had done for him when his father died. Semaun hoped Pak Senik didn't want him to make friends with

Dogol. Dogol had said so many mischievous things about his family. But he could at least promise to leave Dogol alone. If need be, he would avoid quarrelling with him. He could try to forget how Dogol had schemed to burn the family's house down, and to insult his father's spirit. Semaun had one overwhelming desire: he wanted to live in peace and to be treated like a normal human being. He was more directly responsible for the family now. His father, who had been their mainstay for so long, had passed away; his mother was old, and Semek needed his careful attention. He felt a tremendous concern for his sister. Her life must be as untroubled and innocent as possible. She was growing into a woman now. Soon she would leave his care; he wanted to be sure that the right match was made for her.

Pak Senik stood politely when he arrived. Semaun greeted him respectfully and, when he saw Lebai Debasa and Jusoh sitting on the front verandah, did his best to greet them too. He was relieved when they made the proper responses. Pak Senik too was reassured by the general display of goodwill. Semaun took a place in the corner, near the stairs, with his knife resting on his left thigh.

Pak Senik found it hard to know where to begin. He didn't want to hurt anyone. There would be no mention of Dogol at all. Dogol was his responsibility. He would have to go to Dogol's house himself.

'The tiger must die,' he said, opening the discussion.

Nobody said a word.

'Once he's aroused, he'll run wild and turn the whole village upside down,' continued Pak Senik.

Semaun raised his head and nodded, without speaking.

'What do you think, Jusoh?'

'We could shoot it,' Jusoh replied uncertainly.

'We could build a tree-shelter and shoot him. If we dragged the carcase under the tree, old Father Stripes would come the same night; he wouldn't let go of something like that.'

'Whose rifle should we use?' Lebai Debasa suddenly asked.

The intention behind his question was clear. There were only two rifles in Banggul Derdap. One belonged to Pak Senik. The other to Dogol. Pak Senik had no wish to involve Dogol. It was best to leave him alone for a while.

'I think one rifle will be enough. What about you, Semaun?'

Semaun nodded his head, as though that was the only answer he had. He was still silent. It seemed impolite to speak too forthrightly, although he realized that he would be the one to use the weapon. No other youth could shoot in the dark as accurately as he could. He was certainly prepared to wait for the tiger, if Lebai Debasa and Jusoh were willing to help build the shelter. He didn't mind in the least. Pak Senik hopefully studied Semaun's nod. The scheme was difficult, even frightening; all hopes of its success lay with Semaun. The headman knew Semaun was an excellent shot. He himself was too old for that sort of thing. His eyes weren't as sharp as they used to be. Semaun wondered what would happen if Lebai Debasa and Jusoh were tempted to build the shelter too low. It would be no fun being on the same platform as a savage tiger. He wasn't sure he could fully trust Lebai Debasa or Jusoh yet. The youth thought of Semek's beautiful face, as she waited for him to come home.

'Will you help us?' asked Pak Senik.

'Who else will be there?'

'Me. Lebai Debasa. Jusoh.'

'Who'll use the rifle?'

'You can. I'll hold the flashlight. We old men don't see as well as we used to.'

Semaun should have felt very proud. He looked at the

other two guests, trying to decide by their expressions whether they really felt that he could shoot the vicious beast. What if he only wounded it? The tiger would run wild. It could attack the whole village. But if he wasn't prepared to take the rifle, then who would? Pak Senik was too old. His eyesight was failing. Lebai Debasa and Jusoh were old. Their eyesight was no better than the headman's. If he did as they wanted, he might perhaps be able to repay Pak Senik's kindness.

Semaun remained silent. He looked at the three men again. They had never had much confidence in him before. Then, at last, he nodded. Pak Senik smiled. The same smile appeared on Lebai Debasa's and Jusoh's lips. They were all in agreement. Pak Senik would get the villagers to build a platform, and drag the carcase to the trunk of the ironwood tree. The shelter had to be large enough to hold four men: Pak Senik, Lebai Debasa, Jusoh and Semaun. Pak Senik would shine the large, six-battery torch on the tiger. Semaun would shoot it. Lebai Debasa and Jusoh would be there to keep them company and buoy their spirits up.

Although the scheme had been decided on in private, news of it spread quickly. The old people talked about it most. They were all sure that Semaun was capable of shooting the tiger. Nevertheless, many of them disapproved, without any good reason. Most of them would have preferred that Pak Senik shot the tiger. Being old, he would be more careful, they thought.

Although Dogol spent most of his time locked up in his house, he also heard of the scheme.

'It was my cow,' he said to his wife, who had just returned from her parents. 'I should be the one to shoot the tiger.'

'Do you want to kill yourself?' she replied. 'The tiger could leap into the ironwood with no trouble at all.'

'It's my tiger; I should shoot him,' Dogol repeated, as though he had not heard her.

'You'd be killed!' she shouted. Dogol took no notice. He jumped up and walked out of the house. He had to shoot the tiger. The tiger had killed his cow. It was only right he should be the one to shoot it. No one else deserved to. The tiger was no concern of Pak Senik or Semaun. It had nothing to do with Lebai Debasa or Jusoh. The tiger was his; after he shot it, he would drag the corpse out of the forest to Pak Senik's yard. He imagined the villagers swarming around the corpse and himself standing on the tiger's head. Dogol went inside and returned with his rifle. The rifle had an owl trade-mark stamped on it. He snapped it open and inspected the barrel. The metal shone; there was not a speck of dust.

'I'm going to shoot the tiger myself,' he thought, 'without telling anyone. I don't need a platform.' The trunk of the ironwood was three armspans in circumference; he could hide behind it. The tiger would come bounding along, then start tearing and ripping at the cow's flesh, a few feet away from the base of the tree. Dogol would shine his flashlight at the tiger and simultaneously fire a volley of shots. He imagined the tiger leaping into the air, thrashing about with pain and bleeding profusely. He would probably fire a second round, and then a third, before the animal finally fell to the ground, dead.

Strengthened in his resolve, Dogol went back inside the house. His wife was still there.

'I've got to shoot the tiger,' he grumbled at her. She did not reply, but simply stared at him, for a very long while.

It was a terrible night in Banggul Derdap; especially for those villagers with thatched roofs. The sky was pitch black. There was not a single star to be seen. Thunder rumbled now and again, like Satan screaming for a sacrifice. Dogol left his house as the mosque drum announced the second evening prayers. The drumbeat was swallowed by the insane roar of the thunder. No one, except his wife, knew he was going. Fear shone in her eyes as she helplessly watched him walk away. He was quickly lost from sight as the darkness closed around him. For a while she watched the beam of the torch, then that too was gone. He could find his way without it; the maze of small tracks across Banggul Derdap was as familiar to him as the network of veins on the back of his hand. Dogol had been born and raised in the district, and was proud of that.

Dogol arrived somewhat later than the other men. Pak Senik was there first. The four men had not kept the evening prayers; the platform had been finished earlier that day, and they were in their positions by sunset. Semaun held the rifle. Pak Senik was ready with the flashlight. Lebai Debasa and Jusoh listened attentively, ready to draw Pak Senik's attention to the breaking of a branch or a rustle in the undergrowth. The moment they heard anything, Pak Senik was to shine the torch as Semaun aimed his rifle. So far, there had been nothing suspicious. The shrill chatter of the forest was periodically obliterated by the wild rumbling of the thunder. The jungle fowl called out to each other from time to time, but the men ignored them. There was nothing special about the jungle birds; their cries rang constantly over the villagers' heads.

A sudden downpour of rain began lashing at the large trees all around them. The sound of the rain hammering on the dry and fallen leaves on the ground buzzed in their ears. The men were drenched. They smoked in an attempt to forget how cold they were. The ends of their cigarettes glowed brightly each time they inhaled. Dogol was drenched too; he stood at the rear of the ironwood tree, watching them smoke. As he wondered who was sitting in front of the partially covered shelter, he was suddenly overwhelmed by a tremendous hatred for both Pak Senik and Semaun. They were trying to force him out of his own village. The two men in front were al most certain to be Semaun and the headman. Dogol raised his rifle and pointed it at the shelter. He shifted the barrel from side to side, as though deciding which of the two men to shoot first. It was very dark; no one would suspect a thing. He could rush home and pull a blanket over himself before anyone had realized what had happened.

Dogol pressed the butt of the rifle against his shoulder and pointed the weapon at the man on the right of the front of the platform. He didn't know who that was. But if he didn't hit Semaun, he was sure to get Pak Senik. He didn't particularly care whom he shot first.

Just as he was taking aim, he heard an animal treading on the damp leaves. Slowly lowering the rifle, he saw something moving through the darkness. Before Dogol could do anything, Jusoh patted Pak Senik on the shoulder. Pak Senik shone his torch. Two eyes stared at the light. Semaun squeezed the trigger. The tiger jerked and leapt to one side, spitting the cow's flesh from its mouth. Its eyes glared fiercely at the beam of Pak Senik's flashlight. The rain began to pour down once more. The drops beat deafeningly against the dead leaves. Suddenly the tiger saw something move behind the tree. It sprang forwards and broke Dogol's neck. Jusoh heard the scream and immediately patted Pak Senik on the shoulder again. Pak Senik switched his flashlight on. The beam ran backwards and forwards until it struck what it was looking for. The stripes stood out vaguely on the tiger's body. Semaun fired a second time. The animal collapsed to the ground. Pak Senik left the torch on.

'There's someone there!' Lebai Debasa shouted.

Pak Senik shifted the torchlight slightly to the left. The four men gasped when they saw the shape of a human being.

'Get down!' Pak Senik screamed.

'Get down! Get down! Get down!'

They rushed hurriedly down the rough bamboo ladder.
'It's Dogol!' Lebai Debasa called out.
He went over to the corpse.
Jusoh took hold of Dogol and shook him. Dogol's head flopped helplessly backwards and forwards. The rain mingled with the thick blood on his body.
'His neck's broken,' Pak Senik said.
'I probably shot him,' said Semaun guiltily.
'No, you didn't,' replied Pak Senik. 'His neck was already broken.' The old man nodded. Lebai Debasa also nodded in agreement. Jusoh nodded confidently, supporting his two friends.
Pak Senik put his hands on Dogol's head. The driving rain beat sadly against the blood-stained body. A bird called from deep in the forest. The sky was pitch black.
Pak Senik couldn't understand what Dogol was doing behind the ironwood tree. Didn't he know that they were waiting to ambush the tiger? On finding Dogol's rifle by his side, Pak Senik guessed that Dogol had wanted to shoot the tiger before they did. The tiger had broken his cow's neck; he was entitled to his revenge. Why hadn't Dogol fired the first time? He was closer to the beast than they were.
The old man was struck by another thought. Perhaps Dogol had been concentrating on something else at the time. The men on the platform, for instance. Or Semaun, who had now been accepted back into the village. Pak Senik shone his torch carefully on the corpse's face. He studied the eyes and mouth, trying to see if there were any suggestion of a malicious expression. Perhaps Dogol was aiming at them. Pak Senik shivered. It was possible. After all, it was his fault Dogol's ambitions had finally been destroyed. It was his fault Lebai Debasa and Jusoh had turned against Dogol. He had refused to allow Semaun be forced out of Banggul Derdap. He had stopped Dogol setting fire to Semaun's house. There were

many considerations. Pak Senik stood up.

'Let's take the body back,' he ordered. 'We'll leave the tiger here.'

The men at his side nodded.

Later that night, the villagers made their way to Pak Senik's house. The first to arrive was Dogol's wife. Her weeping shattered the evening's silence. The black, overcast sky was briefly lit by the fire-brands which burnt in every corner of Banggul Derdap. The villagers were soaked by the time they reached the headman's house.

Semaun rushed home, but soon returned with his mother and sister.

The body had been laid out in Pak Senik's front room. The room was full of villagers. There was little talk about the accident, which rather surprised Pak Senik. He gave brief answers to their questions. Dogol rushed into the jungle to shoot the tiger, even though he knew they had built the shelter. That was all. He did not tell them what else Dogol had in mind. It was best not to say anything about that. The death had effectively created a new mood in the village. None of the villagers held any grudge against each other now. Semaun had changed. Although he still didn't get on all that well with the other villages, there was nothing to worry about. Pak Senik wanted the village to settle down again as quickly as possible. Only then would he be able to carry through the various projects he had planned.

'Let's go and get the tiger tonight,' one of the villagers shouted. The cry was taken up by several other villagers.

'Let's go and get the tiger!'
'Let's go and get the tiger!'
'Let's go and get the tiger!'

Pak Senik was seated beside the corpse. He chuckled quietly. The combination of their shouting, late at night, and the presence of the dead man, amused him. The villagers apparently considered the tiger more important than Dogol, whose corpse was stretched out in the middle of the room.

'Let's get the tiger!'
'Let's get the tiger!'
'Let's get the tiger!'

The shouting continued. The villagers started fixing their torches again. The flames lit Pak Senik's overgrown front yard. The old man didn't know what to do. He looked at Dogol's wife. She bowed her head.

'Let's get the tiger!' the crowd continued chanting.

Pak Senik walked out of the room to find Semaun. Lebai Debasa and Jusoh were standing nearby; he called them over as well.

'What do you think?' he asked.

'Let them go,' replied Lebai Debasa.

'Will you lead the way?' the old man asked, patting Semaun on the shoulder.

Semaun made no reply. He was ready.

'Jusoh?'

Jusoh nodded.

'Everybody follow Semaun and Jusoh.'

The crowd shouted for joy, as though unaware a man had been killed earlier that night. Although the rain had eased a little, it still persisted. The torches shone brightly. Semaun and Jusoh led the way; they were followed by more than thirty people. The noise was deafening; it continued until they were well into the forest. A sudden quietness fell on Pak Senik's house. Dogol's body lay in the front room. Only a few women had stayed behind.

'We'll bury him in the morning,' Pak Senik said to Dogol's wife. The woman did not look up.

For a long time, they waited in the front room of Pak Senik's house. Then, at last, they caught an indistinct noise in the distance. The shouting was coming gradually closer. The women rushed out onto the bamboo house-platform to see the tiger. Pak Senik went down the stairs and stood in the middle of his yard. A light rain was still falling. The only person left with the corpse was Dogol's wife. An oil lamp flickered gloomily near his head.

They could see the flames of the torches leaping about in the distance. The lights became gradually brighter as they drew closer. Semaun was leading the group. In the middle of the crowd was a rather long object, hanging from a pole. The other villagers waited excitedly for the tiger to arrive. There was complete chaos when Semaun and the group reached the house. They threw the animal down on the ground. Its stripes stood out clearly in the torchlight. The skin would fetch more than a hundred dollars.

'We'll bury it in the morning,' Pak Senik shouted. The crowd around the tiger cheered. Pak Senik went over to Semaun and placed his hand on the youth's sturdy shoulder.

'We'll bury the tiger in the morning,' he repeated. 'We'll bury Dogol then as well. Half of us can bury Dogol, and half of us the tiger.'

The crowd cheered again. It was almost dawn. The villagers kept vigil together until the first rays of dawn shone on the hilltops.